I0649511

Fifty Shades of Chocolate
A Knaughty Experience

Anthony D Green

DEDICATION

This book is dedicated to the lover of words. The ones with the most vivid imagination for passion and everything that comes with it. To those who were looked at as weird or as a freak simply because they voiced something that most would never have the courage to. I know what it feels like to be looked at as different. To be judged by what you say and not by who you are. To be considered as an outsider because you don't conform to what the world thinks you should be. This book is for you. Never be afraid to be you. Chase your dreams, be as creative as you can possibly be, because your mind is incredible!!

ACKNOWLEDGMENTS

Now I have to admit I was a little conflicted at first, but I realized that regardless of the content it wouldn't be me if I didn't give honor to the man above for blessing me with the gift to write. I am forever grateful for my gift. I was told that my gift would make room for me. I am seeing that room form before my eyes.

To my family:
Thank you for always pushing me to be better. There are so many different things I can say helped me to become the man I am. Just know there's no me without you. I can't thank each and every one of you personally because that would take up this entire book. Just know that in this each of you are acknowledged and I love you.

To my friends & poetic family:
Each of you in your own special way have inspired me. Whether it was building the courage to stand on stage and be completely naked in my words, or having the courage to be different, I can honestly say I came into my own around you. A huge part of who I am is because of you.

To **Anthony "AJ Styles" Jones & Taleatha "Blue Lady" Wallace:**
You two are the reason I have this alter ego. AJ you decided to try something different with my hair that ended up being my signature style. Wallace you came up with the name Knaughty so a large part of this goes to you. I thank you for the countless years of support in everything that I do. Words can't describe what you two mean to me. 42 W Lake St in Oak Park, IL will always be my second home. Shout out to the whole AJ Styles family (**Dorene Morrow, Shavella Gunn, Jasmen Welch, and my** big homie **Tiger Lee**)

To the wonderful **Kimberly "Strawberri" Taylor:**
The first time I ever thought about writing an erotic piece was after seeing one of your performances. We met when I was still writing roses are red poems and now I can say that a lot has changed. I thank you for being the one to set the stage for people like me. Thank you for being exceptional. I will forever be grateful for all that you have taught me.

To my Editor **JaRita "Sunshine" Steward:**
Thank you for the countless hours spent making sure this would be a great novel. I am truly grateful. I swear I lost count of the many times you have listened to my crazy ideas and despite how insane you thought they were, you still supported them. That means a lot to me. It's because of you that I found me, and I truly mean that. You've been my friend, my shoulder, my counselor, and at times, my everything. I look forward to addressing you as Dr. Steward really soon, and us working on your best seller.

To **Jessica Vann:**
I can't begin to tell you my gratitude for you. From my cover, to my logo, to my brand, to helping me become more of a business man, I am so grateful. You saw something in me that for a long time I couldn't see in myself and that will be stuck with me forever. We have spent countless hours talking about the future and this empire I'm trying to build. I am lucky to say that because of you I see it forming more than I ever have. The sky isn't the limit for me anymore, I'm trying to take the universe.

To **Courtney Nyree Johnson:**
You have been a pain in my ass, but more than anything else you have been one of my biggest supporters. Each time I wrote a poem you were one of the first people I called or text, and regardless of the time of day you would stop whatever you were doing and listen. You have inspired so much in me that I can't begin to tell you just how thankful I am to have you. Every time I said I couldn't do it you told me I could, every time I wanted to throw the towel in you convinced me not to. You once told me we were in this together and regardless of the distance between us I truly believe that. So I dedicate a part of this book to you, my friend, my pain in the ass, my Nyree!!!

Last but certainly not least I want to thank the wonderful Ms. **Tyomi Morgan**. After several conversations with you I finally understand that the only opinion that should matter is my own. You helped me to see past the opinions, past the judgement, past the side views of others. You helped me to understand that this is a beautiful work of art, and I should take pride in the fact that I'm doing something that most people will never have the courage to do. I admire the woman you are, the free spirit that you possess, and your drive to be different. You are truly an inspiration to me and whether you know it or not you are now my mentor.

Based On A True Story….

THE INTRODUCTION TO SEDUCTION

"Hey babe," Magic's seductive voice floated through the telephone lines, it was the sweetest I'd heard all day.

"Listen, she continued, we've both been so caught up with work and I want us to do something special. So pack a bag babe, I've got something planned to take your mind off work for a while."

"A bag huh?" I chuckled softly, *Damn*, I thought, my baby really knew how to make a brother feel special.

Truth of the matter was I had been working extremely hard. Between mergers and acquisitions there was no time to breathe, let alone enjoy some time with my beautiful wife. We'd only been married a few months and already our jobs had us virtually at opposite ends of the world. I guess that's part of what attracted us to each other, we understood the grind for more. Her as head physician at Mercy Hospital and me and my two companies, time was money. But somehow we managed to keep the spark between us, the one that kept us at each other for the past couple of years. I couldn't get enough of Magic...

"Davin" she asked in a firmer voice, snapping me back to our conversation.

"Yes, baby, I'm sorry I heard you, pack a bag right?"

"Yes, she said in a softer tone, I have an idea. Just follow my instructions, I had my secretary email the address over to you, I'll see you tonight."

Her words held promise, the kind that had me wanting her right then. But before I could share my thoughts she was gone, off to whatever medical emergency that required her attention. Without thinking too deeply into what she had planned I did what I was told.

"Mary, I buzzed my secretary, have Caleb go to the house and grab me some clothes and necessities for the weekend.

"Yes sir. Casual or formal?"

"Both, thank you."

Just as I sat down to get into some reports, my phone buzzed. It was a text from Magic.

I can't wait…I love you.

It was hard to suppress a smile. Shaking my head I tried to get through the pile of work on my desk, I didn't think I'd have a chance to look at it again this weekend.

Driving to meet her I kept thinking about possible things she had planned for us. I wasn't used to being the one wondering, I was a take charge kind of guy. I had to admit though, if only to myself, this bossy shit Magic was pulling, was sexy. Since we were meeting at a hotel, my mind was already on how many ways I could make Magic cum for me. But it was only seven p.m. and knowing my detailed wife I was in for an enjoyable wait. As I pulled up to the hotel I was greeted by the valet.

"Good evening Mr. Davin, your wife is waiting in the lobby for you. Hope you enjoy your stay with us."

We smirked at each other and he gave me a good natured fist bump. Before Magic and I got married we frequented this hotel quite often, it was right in between the hospital and my office, so Thomas the valet knew what it was. We were regulars.

The hotel staff welcomed me warmly as I entered the lobby to find my wife looking sexy as hell, standing under the hotels huge chandelier with a single red rose. She looked amazing and I was already having a hard time controlling myself. I wanted her ASAP.

She was 5'3 with a caramel complexion, curves that would drive a man crazy and the sexiest brown eyes I'd ever seen. All encased in a sexy black dress that had my mind wandering…I'd kissed every inch of that voluptuous body, and I'd be damned if I didn't get a chance to do it again, and soon. We smiled at each other like two young kids in love. I couldn't help but think how lucky I am, though I'm no slouch in the looks department. Magic calls me her favorite kind of chocolate, the dark kind. 5'11 right on the brink of being tall, my fade and goatee were fresh, I had the barber come in on my lunch break to tighten me up and I was still dressed in my black suit, I'd just snatched off the tie in the car and unbuttoned my white shirt for air and to give her a glimpse of my toned, muscular chest. Knowing she was assessing me the way I was her, I sauntered up to her casually until I was standing a few inches away from her looking down into those brown eyes.

"Hey sexy," then I leaned in and gave her a soft lingering kiss, the kind that promised for more.

"Hello husband," she said with a little catch in her breathing that made me smile. She was just as turned on as I was. The anticipation and sexual energy between us was tangible. Her lips parted and I couldn't resist I wrapped her in my arms pressing her body into me, letting my hands find her ass as our lips met. Playfully she bit my bottom lip and moaned into my mouth as I pressed into her harder. Lost in our own bubble of lust, it wasn't until Magic pushed against my chest that I realized people were openly staring at us. "Baby we have to stop, everyone's watching" she whispered with a light giggle. But I didn't care, to be honest I missed her so much. The world could watch if they wanted.

"Come on let's go we have dinner reservations on the rooftop," she said as she grabbed my hand and led me towards the elevator.

Once we got to the rooftop she led me over to a single table with candles set up just for us. "I hope you don't mind, but I wanted it to be just the two of us" she said as she kissed me one more time. Did I mind? Hell no! Immediately I began assessing the different places I could be inside her with this much privacy. This idea had possibilities.

"No baby this is great" I said trying not to let on my thoughts.

"No talk about work, money, or anything dealing with business tonight. This is all about us."

Without a word, I took out my phone and held it up where she could see it as I powered it off. Her answering smile lit me up on the inside. She showed me her empty hands and twirled to prove her phone wasn't with her at all.

Our conversation flowed easily as we ate, relaxing all of the balled up tension from work and the daily rush. She'd known exactly what I needed, and now a completely different kind of tension was building up in me as we flirted over dessert. Everything about her relaxed me, she looked so free and full of joy as the wind blew through her hair. I couldn't help but to stare at her lips, thinking about how bad I wanted to taste them. "Babe" she said startling me out of my thoughts. "Where are you right now" she asked, her forehead crinkling up with concern.

"I'm here baby, right where I need to be."

I stood up, pulling her with me and into my arms. We began dancing slowly, our bodies pressed so close that it was as if we were moving as one. Our eyes connected, filled with growing lust. Her hands moved from my shoulders to my chest while my hands moved from her waist to her ass. We kissed like we invented that shit, losing our breath in the process. She let out several soft moans as I cupped her ass tighter in my hands, letting her feel up close and personal what she was doing to me. She smiled, trailing her hand down my chest and over my torso to caress my dick. Then she started grinding her body up against it, moving her hips back and forth, almost attempting to mount me upright. I leaned into it cupping her ass and pushing her further into me, knowing how it drives her wild.

"Shit Baby you know what that does to me. Don't start something you can't finish she added," seductively meeting my eyes.

"Oh I intend to finish, but you first…" Her eyes widened at my response.

With a huge grin I took her by the hand and led her toward the exit, only stopping to tell the bartender to send a bottle of wine down to our room. Truth was we had enough pull to fuck right on the rooftop without anyone saying a word, but this was my wife, she deserved privacy. Not to mention the shit I hand planned needed special time and attention to detail, the roof just wouldn't do.

As we stood in the lobby waiting on the elevator, I grabbed her by her waist, pulling her close to me and started tugging at the tie keeping her sexy black wrap dress together. She stilled my hand with a smile,

"Not here."

"Don't worry wife, I don't want anyone else seeing what's mine," I said.

Truth be told I wish I didn't have to wait. Hell I wanted Magic right then. Everything about that dress was driving me crazy. I knew under that dress were some of the juiciest breast and the softest ass I'd ever laid hands on. I kissed her once more as the elevator pinged to announce its arrival.

When I saw that no one was in the elevator I gave Magic a sly grin, tugged her inside and up against my body again. Pressing her into the corner I wrapped my hands in her shoulder length brown hair and forced her lips to mine, sucking and nibbling on her lower lip. She returned the favor, devouring my tongue and forcing my pelvis in closer to her with her small hands planted firmly on my ass this time. I couldn't help the smile that lifted the corners of my mouth as my aggressive wife made her needs known. As I assaulted her neck with my tongue, she leaned further into the wall, anchoring one shapely leg around my thigh. Immediately I ran my hand up and down her leg, enjoying the feel of her smooth as satin skin.

Damn she smelled amazing. Whatever fragrance she had on was enticing me all the more. I began tracing my tongue around that spot on her neck slowly, delivering light kisses in the process. Her moans and soft sighs were barely audible at the moment. Finally she hit the button to take us down to the 35th floor. She sucked my lip gently before turning to face the elevator doors. I could see her reflection in the mirrored doors, she was smiling in anticipation.

Surging forward, I pinned her against the doors as we continued our descent. I enticed her with soft kisses to the base of her neck. My hands roamed the outline of her dress until I reached my goal, easing my hand inside, I released the front clasp of her bra and tugged at her nipples gently, still lavishing my agile tongue across her sensitive neck. She pressed her ass into me, moaning, eyes closed, teeth clamped down on her bottom lip. With my free hand I started working my way down the dress to her hips and slowly began sliding the dress up, just enough to place my hand where her legs and ass meet. I could feel her wetness from there and her body was giving off so much heat the doors begin to fog a little.

The wetness on my fingertips made me grow even harder. Suddenly she turned in my arms, wrapping her hands around my neck, she forced my head down to meet her waiting lips, all while gyrating against the swollen bulge inside my pants. I could feel the heat between her legs, she was soft and wet, and I could feel it through my dress slacks. Just as her hand traveled down to loosen my belt buckle the elevator pinged our arrival on the 35th floor. Pulling her dress back down over her hips, I turned my attention to straightening my own clothes and pulled her off the elevator. As soon as we walked into the hallway, she pulled her hand from my grasp and sashayed down the corridor, tossing a haughty smile over her shoulder. I just stood entranced for a moment, my lady was sexy as hell and such a fucking tease. That dress had to come off…I might let her leave on those sexy 6 inch stilettos though…

"Are you coming," she asked, pausing at the door to our room. When I hesitated again, she crooked a finger at me.

"Not yet baby, but I plan on it," I replied with a smug smile.

LOOSE CONTROL

Come to me so I can help you relax your mind.
Allow time to get lost in us.
Let lust get jealous of what we share.
We possess something so rare
that us being here changes the dynamics of our fate.
Having you here shows me you were worth the wait,
because I feel like I've waited a lifetime.
Allow me to help you unwind,
close your eyes, and let the music soothe you.
There are so many things I want to do to you,
but I'm all about pleasure first.
Tell me every place on your body that hurts
so I can massage away the pain.
Allow my hands to send signals to your brain
that tells you that you're safe.
Travel to a place where ecstasy is no longer an illusion,
a place of orgasmic seclusion,
a place where moans will be the only form of communication
we're using.
I'm talking fusing our minds together
so our thoughts write love letters for each other.
Let each stroke form the perfect note,
I'm trying to provoke your mental,
so I'll massage your temples til there nothing left in you to think
about.
Allow my fingers to trace the outline of your mouth

and plant kisses each time a word tries to come out.
Right now there's no need for words.
Every thought your body screams out is heard loud and clear.
Let me draw you near, bury my face in your neck,
and take in everything I have here with me right now.
I want to understand how your scent has me spent,
so I gently lick to capture it's wonderful taste.
Let me travel to a familiar place that stands erect like statues,
but hold so much substance and value.
I'm ready to devour you,
but instead I'll gently suck.
I feel your chills rush through your body
as you erupt from this light pressure.
This auspicious gesture only brings more pleasure.
I want to get to know you better
than any man has ever taken the time to.
I want to subdue every part of you
so I'll slowly continue my decent.
I want you to cherish every moment spent,
every touch, every lick, every kiss I plant.
I want to do something most can't,
and that's take my time.
I want to uncover the buried treasure you're trying to hide,
let my hands glide along your sides as I slide down deeper.
Mmmmm, Even your sweat is sweeter
than anything I've ever had before.
I want more so I explore your lower extremities.
I feel your hands feeling me as I trace circles down your thighs.
You spread your legs open wide ready to let me inside
but now is not the time so I don't oblige.
I keep moving,
take your foot in my hands and start soothing
every area that's tense.
I make sure no area is missed
and once I'm done with this I place each toe in my mouth,
slowly, not enough for it to tickle
and you have to take it out.
I want to tease before I please,
make you tense before I ease.

I know exactly what you need,
just lay back and let me lead,
and I promise you'll love my direction.
I'm all about perfection,
and they say practice makes perfect,
so I do it slow because you're worth it.
Your body was created to be worshiped,
so I bow down and give praise for this beautiful gift I was given
as I planted a seed in your soul.
Did I turn you on?
Did I make you lose control?

THE SEDUCTRESS

As she stood in the hall, giving me that seductive look over her shoulder, signaling me to join her, I stood in the doorway of the elevator trying to act unfazed. But who the hell was I kidding, shit everything about her walk turned me on more. The seductive movement of her ass in that dress made me want to be inside of her that very second. With renewed purpose I started walking towards her, eyes focused on her perky ass.

Once we were at the room door, she reached in her bra to grab the key card. Coming up behind her quickly, I pushed my body against hers, taking her voluptuous frame into my arms and began kissing the base of her neck, inching around to her earlobe. That always set her off, I knew my baby's triggers like the back of my hand. Softly I pulled her earlobe into my mouth, sucking and biting it until she half giggled, half moaned in response. My cock twitched in answer, this is what I'd been waiting for all Dam day. Sliding my hand across her dress, unable to wait any longer I slide my hand beneath the folds of her wrap dress.

Hands still at work I looked around to make sure no one was in the hallway as I slide my fingers down her belly and between her legs. My eyes half closed in anticipation as I found her lace panties.

"Damn Baby."

Tracing the line of her thigh, I slid my hand into her panties and began stroking her soft skin as she leaned into my fingers, moaning. Sliding my fingers through her warm waiting folds, I started circling my fingertips around her pulsating clit. Damn she was wet as hell. Her breaths started coming in faster, shallower pants.... I could feel the anticipation building....

Taking my other hand from its resting place on her belly, I took the key card out of her hand and slid it into the room door.

Once the light turned green I quickly turned the handle and we slid into the room with an urgency that belied our passions. Slamming the door behind me, I gave a quick tug to the sash holding her dress, leaving it gaping open. Smiling seductively she slid the dress off her shoulders and stood looking at me with heat in her eyes. I took in the black lace bra and panties she was wearing,

"Damn Magic."

Before I could say anything else we were at each other, bodies suddenly magnetized together as we kissed intensely, lips to lips, tongues battling intensely in a game that would wield two winners in the end. Magic nibbled on my bottom lip, as my hands reached around to palm her juicy ass, MY juicy ass.

There was absolute silence between the two of us, just moans and the wet sounds of our lovemaking. Suddenly Magic pulled back and began unbuttoning my shirt, she made quick work of it and slid her hands across my chest, pushing my shirt off my shoulders and onto the floor. With a wicked smile she grazed her nails across my chest and bit into my nipples, sucking and pulling at them softly. My eyes drifted shut, taking it all in.

The more she bit into me the more I whispered "Harder" as my thoughts drifted into complete submission.

Soon she was biting lower and lower until she was on her knees. I came back to reality with a start, eyes fluttering open as I felt her begin to unfasten my belt. As she pulled the belt from my pants she began kissing my stomach.

"Damn, damn, damn" was all I could say as she looked up at me with that mischievous smile.

Unzipping my pants she slid them and my boxers down in a smooth motion

"Relax baby" she said as she worked her way back up my body. "Relax" I said questioningly, in between breaths. Who the hell could relax at a time like this? Magic had me hard as hell and ready to attack her, but I'd play along for now, I'd let her have her way, for now.

As she got back up to face me I grabbed her, pulling her in close, Sliding my tongue across her lips I ran my fingertips along her spine, making her tremble in my embrace. Not wanting to waste any more time, I unsnapped her bra to reveal the most perfect pair of breast and they were all mine to admire. Before she could get a word out I latched onto her nipple, sucking and biting until she couldn't contain herself. Moaning loudly she ground her hips into me as I flicked my tongue around her hardened nipples, repeating the action on each breast.

I was vaguely aware of her hands sliding down my back to cup my ass with small petite fingertips. My dick was already hard as hell, waiting on her to do whatever it was she was going to do to it. She ran her hands up from my ass, around my waist to take my pulsating dick in her hands and began stroking the hell out of it. I could tell it wouldn't be long now. She then slid down to her knees again and took my penis in her mouth seductively sucking it vigorously.

"Oh Fuck" I said trying not to show what she was doing to me "Slow down babe". She paused looking up at me with a smile

"Don't tell me how to handle my dick" with that she began her assault again, alternating between long slow strokes and fast, deep strokes.

Who the fuck was I kidding? Magic was about to unman me and I was biting my lip, doing all I could to hold in the building moans as my cock hardened to the fullest extent. Stepping back, to compose myself I started kicking off my shoes and unwrapping my pants and boxers from my ankles. Magic fake pouted because I'd taken her chocolate treat from her, but moved to slide out of her panties as well. I paused to watch her as her breasts dangled forward with her movements. I'd always thought I was an ass man…that is until I'd met her.

My wife had some of the juiciest breast and sexiest nipples I'd ever put my mouth on. I couldn't contain myself anymore, I picked her up, hands palming her ass and carried her over to the bed, kissing and licking her lips on the way. It was time to end this agony and give her what we both wanted. As I laid her on the bed she looked up at me so fucking sexy and whispered,

"I want you inside me, now."

At that moment my hard dick seemed to twitch in response.

With a smile I simply said, "Ride it."

KAMA SUTRA

Let's set the scene
One summer's eve
cool breeze
Sweet melodies
serenade the night
the light was just right
Blindfolds to cover sight
Satin to make ties tight
Tonight I want to seduce you
Introduce you
To the naughtiest karma sutra
You've ever seen
First let's gets you clean
With a nice bubble bath
Then commence to remove
Every article of clothing you have
Tonight it's all on me
Let the water do the soothing
A little music for grooving
A lite breeze for cooling the skin
As I place your foot in my hand
To be careful where I'm touching
Clean toes are meant for sucking
But I won't go there yet

I lather what's wet
Feet to neck
Back to breast
Then a rinse before I dry you off
Damn your skin is soft
But I can't get lost
Time to move ahead
Bath to bed
In a room that's candle lit
With the sweetest fragrance
I need you to be patient
There's pleasure in waiting
So with no hesitation
I oil you down
You release the sweetest sounds
As I massage what's tense
Nothing's missed
A kiss to lips
Before my tongue takes trips
To other regions of you
A tongue pleasing is due
An over and through
Before I subdue
The sweetest spot
That little knot
The one that makes hot an understatement
An ultimate salivating
Just for you
Just want to get it wet for you
But no ordinary wet would do
I want to drown in it
Have a constant reminder
every time I'm down in it
Buried treasures can be found in it

So I dig deeper
The further in it gets sweeter
Till you scream that's it
One last flick
As I lift
I'm talking neck surrounded by hips
Just to take it all in
Moans and name calling
Before falling back to the bed
And that was just the head
As I flip you over
Hand grips to shoulders
The ultimate form of controlling
The best way of holding you
If you knew what this hold could do
I suggest you get ready
Pulsating heavy
Release the levy
And let it fall down
Call out
Let it all out
Till you can't speak
climax with me
But know we've only begun
This was just a sample of round one.....

SEDUCED

Her eyes widened in anticipation as I laid back on the bed next to her. Suddenly her look transformed into that of a lioness about to pounce on her prey. She began making her way down my body, leaving a trail of kisses. Once she reached my hard dick she straddled me, easing down on it slowly. I couldn't help but tip my head back into the bed, eyes closed in pleasure; she felt so good, so tight... This was home.

She was being careful only taking half of me in at first, then with a slow intensity she began grinding her hips into me, and the more she ground her hips the more the walls of her pussy opened, letting all of my girth in, inch by inch. Moaning and tossing her head back, she dug her nails into my chest, taking every inch and grinding into me. I met her thrust for thrust, our bodies rippling together in perfect harmony. She moaned and dug her nails into my chest. "Oh fuck Davin, oh shit" she moaned as she leaned forward and continued grinding her clit against me. She then began grinding harder and faster.

I could tell she was about to cum so I sat up a little and began sucking her nipples. "Ooooo shit baby," she moaned louder as she slightly lifted herself up and slammed back down on it. The harder she slammed down the louder she moaned until "Shit, baby I'm about to cum" she cried out. "Cum for me baby, cum only on this dick babe," almost immediately after I said it, I felt a flood of wetness all over me.

But she wasn't done. With only the briefest of pauses she began to buck harder than before but with renewed energy. Her pace quickened with a faster up and down motion. She felt so damn good on top of me as I held her hips to push myself deeper inside her. I could feel her pussy tighten up on my dick once again before she released another loud cry and squirted all over my dick.

I reached up and squeezed her tits as she continued riding the hell out of me. She was climaxing in what felt like an endless torrent, the feel of her muscles pulsing around my cock were almost enough to take me over the edge. The bed soon became soaked beneath us with the evidence of her orgasms. After four explosions of heat, wetness and those tight walls she looked down at me nearing her end.

With a devilish smirk, I flipped her over onto her back, then turned her again positioning her with that luscious ass in the air. Arching her back and pointing her toes just the way I liked, she looked behind her with a haughty smile before leaning lower into the bed. She knew this was my favorite position. I looked down at that big juicy ass and that wet monkey that I'd just shaved bald a couple nights ago and said,

"I don't think I've pleased my wife enough just yet….let me remedy that."

Magic's eyes widened as I dove in, put my face in between her thighs, pressed right against her ass, I started flicking my tongue lightly over her clit, slow strokes meant to drive her insane. Moaning, she pressed her ass into my face, loving it, I put both hands up, spread her cheeks to get a better angle on that wet pussy and went to work. After the flicking sent her squirming, I started sucking that sensitive nub soft and then harder, trying to suck the juices right out of her body, until she went limp with the sensation. Finally one last time I just laid my tongue on her clit, removing one hand from her ass, to stick two fingers into her wet folds.

She jerked forward in surprise, but I held on with my right hand on her ass, all of a sudden Magic's cries built to a point of desperation before she shattered around me a quivering wet mess. I caught every juicy drop on my tongue, licking up and around her pussy to make sure I got it all. Without even pausing to let her collect herself, I slid into her effortlessly, feeling the after-shocks that my tongue had caused. Her insides quivered on my dick and I just sat and let the orgasms shake through her, squeezing me oh so pleasantly. Finally I started stroking her, slowly lingering on the pull out and swirling my hips on the way back in.

I wanted her to have every inch of this hard dick. Then I would pull out slowly, until the head was barely inside her, quickly sliding back in again. I kept this alternating rhythm up, each time going a little faster than before. "Harder baby" she moaned into the pillow she was gripping as I wrapped my hands around her waist and quickened my pace. The more she moaned, the more I felt her pussy tighten up around my dick. My body was in hyper speed fucking the shit out of her sweet pussy, feeling each and every orgasm that shook her.

Feeling like I was going to go straight through her I stroked and stroked as she threw that ass back, knuckles turning white on the pillow as she muffled her moans in the mattress. I felt my end drawing near, pulling a hand back from her waist I smacked her ass and watched it bounce back on me. Unable to hold it Magic let out a loud cry of ecstasy.

"Fuck, I'm cumming too babe."

Arching her back just a little more she said, "cum on love."

I lost it and I felt my body release, pouring inside her all the pent up sexual tension of the day. Magic's whole body vibrated beneath me with the aftershocks of her orgasm. Pulling out of her slowly, I laid next to her, sweaty and exhausted we laid on the bed staring at one another. I could tell this was the release that we both needed. But it wasn't just a release for me.

"Damn baby" Magic said trying to catch her breath as she wiped the sweat from her face "that was everything".

I couldn't help but smile because she was reading my mind completely. "Yeah baby it was" I said as I kissed her breast, "I needed this more than you know". The satisfied look on her face told me she already knew that. "Baby" Magic moaned seductively. "Yes" I said already knowing what was about to happen as she took my still pulsating dick in her hands preparing to suck it. "You ready" she said as she laid in-between my legs. I smiled, gripping her head "Are you"……

RIDER

You walk into the room
Mind consumed with what I'm about to do
I'm talking a round for round bout with you
No Floyd so there won't be any running
Only one direction and that's you cumming
You've been summoned
Put your gloves on
It's time to get our grudge on
So be prepared to get knocked down
First pants...
Wait gone remove them socks now
Tongue to your spot now
Soft slow flicks before I drop down
Only one spot in mind
I'm on something different
So let me get it from behind
Chin resting on your thighs while inside
Let's play a game
Hands to Cola frame
The Coco makes me go insane
So I savor the flavor
Licking makes it greater
No worries of later
I plan to devour you now
Paint a masterpiece by mastering
The art of my mouth
And you can be my canvas
My actions are candid

I plan to see you dancing
But in a different way
than you're accustomed to
Simply from me touching you
You'll wind with a slow grind
While I'm clutching you
And I'll suck what's suckable
Till you fall out
Or your juices run all out
But I prefer the latter
Pleasure is all that matters
We'll worry about the rest after
So tell me can you handle this
Strokes from my oversized candle stick
With plans to flick
Till your flame goes out
I promise more pleasure
than pain goes south
Buck till your frame goes out
Just don't change routes
Ride till your name's called out
Or until I'm done
Bounce for fun
Make it numb
When I cum
Don't run
This is what you wanted
You said my dick was your opponent
And you'd hop on it
until it concedes
Make me tap out
Make me sleep
Make me believe
You got what it takes
I got a prize for you
And not a drop needs to go to waste....
Let's get ready to rumble!!!!

SWEET AFTERNOON

Cherie' sat in her office with tension singing throughout her body. Rotating her neck this way and that she tried to shake off the tight feeling in her gut. Squirming in her seat searching for a more comfortable position, she tried to go back at her financial reports again.

"Focus Cherie'," she chided herself aloud.

Narrowing her eyes at the computer screen, she tried to tackle the reports again. Not five minutes later the screen began to blur in front of her and the squirming started all over. This wasn't working. Restlessly, she toyed with things on her desk, shifting her stapler, wiping off none existent dust, stacking and moving papers; jumping up with a frustrated sigh she walked briskly over to the window of her office, and pulled it open a few inches. The air felt good on her heated skin, blowing back her shoulder length brown hair and ruffling her blouse. Pulling off her suit jacket and laying it on the chair next to the window, Cherie' began rotating her shoulders to release the tension. Rubbing her tender neck, she closed her eyes, letting the breeze drift over her and her thoughts wander.

It had been 2 months since Cherie' and Jamal had said their vows. Her friends had laughed at her when she'd told them the two of them had decided to wait until after they were married to well...consummate their relationship. Jamal was fine, 6'2, with a basketball players build all muscular upper arms, trim waist and firm abs. He had the sincerest brown eyes, full lips, framed by a neat goatee and a head full of waves that would make you seasick. The waiting had been almost unbearable at times, but they'd fought through it, wanting to make sure that this time intimacy would mean a lifetime. After their gentle, passionate wedding night, their cravings for each other had only increased. The waiting had seemed to strike a match that had them both insatiable, it had been hard to leave the bed for weeks after, hell even now it was hard to leave him in the morning...hence her problem. Two in the afternoon and she was in heat....again. Even though her body was still tender from this morning's activities...had it really only been five hours ago that she'd lay next to him, spent and floating on a cloud from their lovemaking? Now here she was again flushed with the need for her new husband. The way his lips grazed across her neck, then baring teeth and nibbling at her collar bone and breasts and lower...

"Get a hold of yourself, woman!" She chastised herself aloud, casting away her X-rated thoughts. Reaching over to close the window, Cherie' made up her mind that she was going to get some work done.

"Get a hold of what Cher?"

The deep familiar voice made her jump, turning from the window quickly, she came face to face with the object of all of her pent up desire.

"Jay," she breathed.

The light in her eyes and smile on her face showed her husband just how happy she was to see him. He smiled back, amused and pleased, before crossing the room quickly, and scooping her into his arms for a full body hug that sent Cherie's body right back on its wayward spiral. As if he could feel her desire he pulled back slightly to look down into her brown eyes.

"I missed your sexy ass."

He accented his words with an aggressive hand on her behind, pushing her hips into his. Jamal had a deep, husky tone to his voice that sent tingles up and down Cherie's spine every time she heard it. Closing her eyes briefly, hands tightening on his waist, she allowed herself to melt into the feel of his hard body and his hard dick, pressed right up against her belly. Cherie' was 5'5 to his 6'2, but her 4 inch heels allowed her to rest her head on his chest, right under his chin. Taking a deep breath and exhaling to release the sexual heat building between her thighs, she opened her eyes about to speak when Jamal's mouth descended on hers, taking and giving until she melted into him.

God he had a sexy mouth!

His thick lips were firm and warm on hers. Jamal still had his hands on her ass pushing her into him as he invaded her mouth. Before Cherie' could gather her thoughts, Jamal began hiking up her pencil skirt, exposing her full ass and thick thighs. Absently Cherie' thought how glad she was she'd worn some of the underwear she'd gotten from her Bachelorette party....good times. Suddenly Jamal's hands stilled, he stepped back for a minute, assessing his wife with a hungry gaze. Cherie' smiled, absently wondering if he'd locked the door. She didn't want her secretary to come back from lunch and be scandalized.

As if reading her mind, Jamal walked over to the door and locked it. Casually he took his suit jacket off and laid it on one of the chairs facing her desk. Then he took his phone out of his pocket, puzzled, she watched as he flipped through his phone, before finally brushing past her to set it on her desk. Cherie' couldn't resist the huge grin that overtook her face as Avery Sunshine's Sweet Afternoon began to play through the speakers on her desk. With her back turned to her husband she slipped out of her pencil skirt and pulled off her blouse, letting it drop to the floor slowly. Still standing with her back facing him, Cherie' was filled with the eroticism of standing in nothing but her lacey underwear in her place of business.

Jamal stood leaning against her desk, taking in his sexy wife.

"Damn" he whispered.

Taking in her luscious ass, thick thighs and shapely legs. Cherie' had on a lacey red bra, red panties and stockings with fucking…what were they called? Oh Garters, hell fucking yeah, his wife was the shit.

Loosening his tie, Jamal walked up behind his wife as she posed seductively, hip cocked, back arched how he liked it…coming up behind her he ground his hips into her ass and reached around to cup her full breasts, letting them fill his hands. Leaning back into him, Cherie' reached up to pull his head down to hers. Squeezing her nipples as they kissed, Jamal felt himself getting harder, until his dress pants were an uncomfortable restraint. Flipping around in his arms, Cherie grabbed his growing penis and gave it a playful squeeze, before making quick work of his pants and shirt. Jamal kicked off his shoes, freeing himself completely and lifted her by her thighs.

Cherie eagerly responded wrapping her legs around his waist, plastering her mouth to his in a kiss that had her lips tingling and her insides clenching in anticipation. As he moved toward her desk she absently wondered if she had anything important on it, then her backside touched the desk sending a cold jolt through her as her bottom touched the cold surface. Jamal stood in between her legs, rock hard against her belly. He grabbed her by her hair, kissing her hard before going to work on her garters. Before he could work her garters down, Cherie' slid off the desk and took him into her mouth, sucking him deep to the back of her throat and beyond.

PLEASURE ZONE

We share more ties than shoes laced
We've stood in a place
Were space didn't exist
Took trips
To places missed
Between these lips of ours
the quickest route to my heart
Rest in her arms
So she holds me
Kisses me slowly
She knows me
I'm desired and she shows me
How real it gets
Pecks from the softest lips
I've ever tasted
Now any other lips would be tasteless
My tongue's eager to taste it
The desire is so strong
I just want to suck and hold on
To savor the flavor she has
But would she be mad or enjoy it
Would she read the signs
Of where this is going
I'm exposing another side of me
Will she take this ride with me
Go inside with me
And not come out for hours
We're connected
so we're exchanging power
She climbs me like a tower
Tells me to devour
Before I go in

Tongue so deep my nose is in
Her cries I win
Thighs to chin
Then rise up
Sized up
So I know what needs to happen
Turn and bend to see her reactions
Arching her back is her reaction
She's prepared for insertion
Not afraid of it hurting
Moans and light squirting
While I'm working
She goes berserk when I go deeper
The sensation gets sweeter
I'm merely trying to free her
From herself
She begs for help
Her orgasm is felt
So I give her mine in return
We collapse in passion from pleasure earned

MIDDAY PLEASINGS

Pulling slowly back, glancing up at his stunned face she began to work in a sensual rhythm, tightening her lips around him at the tip and sucking him deep over and over until his head fell back and he gripped her shoulders. Just as she felt him hardening to the point of release she quickened her motions, but Jamal growled low in his throat, pulling back, with quick movements he hoisted her off the floor and pressed her back on the desk, scattering everything left and right. Before Cherie' could think if anything important had fallen his mouth was on her wet pussy, gentle at first flicking across her sensitive nub until she was squirming for more. Planting his hands on her thighs, he pulled her clit into his mouth and started a light sucking that continued to increase in intensity. Reese felt herself climbing, gripping his head desperately she arched her back and let her head fall back stifling the desire to scream as he sent her plunging over the edge in a pulsating torrent of wet heat.

Before she could fully come down, he plunged his tongue inside her exploring her walls, tasting her juices before going back to the tantalizing torture of her clit.

After the third orgasm, Cherie' was begging for Jamal to be inside her. Rising slowly, licking his lips seductively, letting her know how good she tasted; he pulled her body down to the edge of the desk, hoisted her legs up onto his hips and plunged inside her, causing her body to lift up even higher off the desk in ecstasy. She was overcome with his warmth and strength, so much so that she almost climaxed again, but as if sensing it he pulled out hastily, circling the tip of his length at her opening and then sliding into her swiftly again. Jamal's hands guided her by her waist and Cherie' dug her nails into his arms, loving the feel of him moving in and out of her circling his hips and making her crazy with need.

Slowly she began to build again and Jamal feeling her tightening around him slowed down, pulled back and placing his thumb at her sensitive clit began to mimic the movements of his hips with his hands. The double assault sent Cherie' into orbit again, stars, fireworks exploding in her vision causing her to tremble and convulse. Jamal's head fell back in bliss as her wetness and clenching walls crushed down on his dick in the sweetest way, jolting his hips into an accelerated rhythm. Feeling his coming climax, she thrust her hips back into him, meeting him thrust for thrust, coaxing him to release. But Jamal wasn't having it, he was a fucking tease and Cherie' pouted as he pulled out of her, gathering himself.

He was trying to savor this shit, but Cherie' wanted his release just as much as her own. Pushing him back, she hopped off the desk and turned, bending over it, ass arched in the air, waiting… Jamal groaned, he'd come here to tease his wife, make her cum, but she was dead set on taking him with her and he wasn't in the mood to resist. Grabbing her hips aggressively, Jamal positioned himself and slid into her with only the slightest bit of resistance, his inexperienced wife was still acclimating to his girth.

Slowly Jamal began pumping into her, and dam if she wasn't throwing it back like the shit wasn't phasing her. Jamal couldn't help himself, as his wife covered her mouth to stifle her own moans, one hand clenching the far end of the desk, he picked up pace, knowing he was about to lose it.

With a strangled groan, Jamal spilled into Cherie' filling her up with his warmth, and she took all of it, shivering with pleasure. Leaning forward Jamal rested his head on her back, rubbing his hands up and down her hips and thighs, still rooted inside her.

Kissing her softly he said, "this has been on my mind all damn day."

Unable to help it she laughed out loud, "Baby me and you both."

After a moment they both gathered themselves and dressed quickly. Wrapping his arms around Cherie', Jamal kissed her slowly, before pulling back and smiling at his wife,

"We should have more afternoons like this."

"It was definitely sweet," Cherie' said, referencing the song still on repeat.

Jamal smiled, gave her ass a light squeeze and sauntered out the door, greeting her secretary with a smug smile on the way out. This was definitely one sweet afternoon for the both of them and it was going to be an even sweeter evening.

CONQUEST

We made love
Intertwined more than just physical parts
Bodies close enough to stitch our hearts
We shared passion
Gave more than just physical action,
Climaxing, ass smacking, tongue lashings, and sheet grabbing
We gave emotions
Penetrating penetrations we penetrated barriers most couldn't
reach.
Students to the art so we both couldn't teach
She rides
Glides more than thighs to relieve desires inside
She strides
while cries of pride bellow from her larynx
We stare
Then kiss as flood gates open
We speak
With no words spoken
One more stoke and she's provoked to finish
Never have I had a more perfect ending
This is only the beginning
The night we made love
Now every time we touch

we get a sweet rush
so we rush to a place
where sweet lust could meet us
and we're right back in it
I pick up where she finished
created a beginning the first time
Followed my first mind and devoured her
that empowered her once again to take control
She played the role of director
directing directions to get her to fall in
I'm all in so she knows my poker face
I know the place we're headed
forgetting our environment
we spark so our fire gets ignited
her body invited inviting feelings
feeling every part of her
damn she's soft but I'm hard for her.......

WORKDAY PLAY

Dam, she was sexy. Sometimes I caught myself starring after her fine ass after she walked away. But she was my boss and this shit was out of line right? It all started with casual, friendly conversation, every day we'd shoot the shit. Then I started testing the waters, just to see what her boundaries were. First it was playful names starting with, "hey love," and then escalating to a whispered "hey sexy," every now and then. She'd responded to! "Hey Chocolate," she'd say and it would move me in just the right kind of way you know?

So I would tell her how beautiful she was today and she'd give me that seductive smile then bat her eyelashes at me. Dam she had some beautiful eyes... Chrissy was everything a brother like me wanted and more. But as luck would have it she was still my boss and the rules against work relationships were severe. After a while though I really didn't give a fuck, shit I just wanted to fuck Chrissy, plain and simple. We had a chemistry that was electric and I was dying to see what she tastes like. From her responses I could tell she was on the same shit.

Tired of the back in forth I said fuck it and decided to shoot my shot. From the poetic quotes and artwork she had hanging up in that big ass office of hers I could tell that she loved the arts, so I decided to push her imagination as far as I could. Best way to a woman is to stimulate her mind, the body will follow soon after. I'm not much of a poet but I thought I'd send her a message, describing what I wanted to do to her, in clever, poetic disguise. I knew my little erotic snippet was sure to leave her wanting more.

I want to greet you before the sun has the chance to rise,
Offer more than just an occasional surprise;
be the best part of your rise
when you wake up.
Never been one to need a cup,
I'll sip from you.
Besides the best cream I get is from you
and from the looks of it there's a surplus;
so I'm curious just how much I can slurp up.....

I hit send on the message before I could change my mind. I shot my shot, hopefully I wouldn't get slapped or fired for my horny bullshit. My Cubicle isn't too far from her office, I can see right through the blinds by just rolling back my chair an inch or two. So I knew when she got the message, her eyes lit up and I could almost see the flush spread across her cheeks. She finally looked up at me with the most peculiar look on her face. Somehow I could tell she was intrigued. Maybe it was the flush in her cheeks or the way she squirmed in her seat as we made eye contact. What happened next was totally unexpected, she looked down suddenly and began typing quickly. The ding of the messenger on my computer surprised me and I jumped lightly. Scooting my chair up to the desk quickly, I opened the message to find one sentence, but it made her thoughts blatantly clear.

When do you want your coffee?

That shit caught me so off guard I dam near fell out of my chair. I looked up quickly to see if she'd noticed and sure enough she was stifling giggles with her hand. Hell I wanted her ass now, my dick was getting hard thinking about it, but I decided to leave her wanting. I didn't reply to her message. I set back to work, but I was distracted as hell the whole day, trying to keep myself calm so I wouldn't bust through my dam pants.

As the days turned into weeks the tone of our dialogue changed from casual flirting to downright nasty. She'd comment on my dick print in every pair of pants I wore, and I'd ask about the color panties and bra set she had on daily. I'd tell her I wanted to bend that ass over her desk and she'd tell me she wanted to deep throat my dick. The verbal foreplay had me walking around with a permanent hard on, but we never touched. Not even accidently. We were very careful of that and somehow it made our game play all the more intense. Every day was something different, but every day she made me want her more and more. I had to talk myself down from rubbing my dick behind the small barrier that was my cubicle on more than one occasion. That sassy mouth of hers made me want to walk right across the office and fuck her in front of everybody. I'd be unemployed, but that release just might be worth it.

What I had been longing for finally came one Friday night. It was around 7 and most of the staff had left for the day. I was stuck in the office trying to finish up a big project that was due Monday morning. I honestly thought I was the only one in the office. That is until I looked at my computers messenger and saw that she was still logged in. I decided to message her and find out what she was doing there this late. I could hear the ding that let me know my message had went through. She was in her office with the lights off, probably so no one would bother her.

The ding resounded through the empty office as her response lit up on my screen. Her message simply said, finishing up some work. I replied back immediately wanting to test the waters.

Your ass looked amazing in that dress today...what kind of

panties you got on?

I heard her giggle lightly and then the faint tapping of computer keys as she responded.

Red lace thong, with a matching bra. I wore the dress for you...and the underwear.

I closed my eyes, envisioning her in just that thong and bra. Chrissy was about 5'3, honey complected, with a frame that had to be sculpted by an erotic Goddess. She was known as the eye candy by most of the guys in the office. Everyone wanted her but if I was lucky, I'd be the one to get that ass. Snapping out of my thoughts with a shake of my head, I messaged her back.

Let me see...

Her response was immediate, "*sure.*"

I paused briefly, but unable to resist any longer, I stood up and looked toward her offices, she was typing, still looking back and forth between her computer screen and whatever reports were in her hand. Without thinking I threw my papers down and headed purposefully toward her office. As if she felt me coming, she looked up, I caught her eye through the doorway and she seemed to freeze in place, fingers still on the keyboard, papers clutched a bit too tightly in her hand. Somehow this emboldened me. The way her luscious lips were parted I knew she wanted me just as bad as I wanted her. Feeling the need to savor the moment, I stopped and leaned against the door frame. We looked at each other in silence for what seemed like hours, when she finally straightened her back, put her papers down, leaned back in her chair and crossed her legs, hands playing with the expensive pendant around her neck.

Licking her lips slowly she said, "is there anything I can help you wit…"

Before she could get the last word out of her mouth, I was on her, crossing the room so fast I don't remember how I got there; but there I was scooping her up out of the chair she was sitting in. She froze a minute caught off guard before wrapping her body around mine in a hot, wet kiss. I invaded her mouth with my tongue like I was devouring her from the inside out. Pulling back briefly I tossed her on the desk and slid everything off of it with a careless brush of my arm. With my hands at her waist I moved in between her legs, looking down to watch her skirt hike up around her waist. Looking up my dark brown almost black eyes met her honey brown eyes, I wanted to make sure she was still down for the ride....she was. So I took my right hand and traced the outline of her neck allowing my fingers to descend to her plump and juicy ass breast. Damn they felt great inside my hand. I squeezed her firmly and she let out a sweet, faint moan. I could feel her nipples hardening as I started to tug at them, pulling lightly and then pinching harder.

Leaning into my hands, Chrissy was panting for air, as her lips parted I leaned down to devour her again, enjoying the warm wetness of her mouth. I felt her body shiver from the initial kiss as she wrapped her legs around my waist. She jumped a little at the feel of my throbbing dick against her warm thighs. I smiled down at her and with a sly grin she started tracing the outline in my pants. More turned on than I'd ever been I leaned down and kissed her again, trying to bury myself in her, with one hand on her breasts and the other on her ass pushing her closer in to me.

My hands began sliding down the length of her dress, down far enough for me to get a good grip on it in order to take it off her. She kicked off her 5 inch black pumps, and lifted her arms up for me to get the dress completely off, before tossing it in the corner along with those sexy ass pumps she'd had on. Canvasing her body I could see that bra and that thong she described to me earlier in the messages. Her body was amazing. I knew I couldn't wait any longer. The anticipation alone damn near made me bust.

Leaning in to her, using my tongue to trace her neck, biting as I licked, sucking as I went lower, hands traveling all over her body, down to grip that soft yet plump ass of hers, I could feel her losing control as the moments passed. Unsnapping her bra, kissing her breast, sucking her pierced nipples, listening to her let off moans, I could feel her succumb to me. She was open for anything and everything at this moment. But I wanted this to be an orgasmic experience that she would remember each time she sat in the office, let alone at this desk. I was going to make sure she always wanted to stay late after work.

Unable to stand the constant teasing any longer, Chrissy quickly unbuttoned my pants, unzipped them, and pushed them down as far as she possibly could. My engorged dick resting hard as hell inside my boxer briefs. She grabbed it, let off a half growl, half moan and pulled me closer to her, pressing the head of my dick into her thong. I could feel how wet she was. I could feel the pulsating from her clit. She was ready to be fucked right now.

Lifting my hand from her breasts I quickly pushed her thong to the side, her eyes widened in anticipation. There was nothing she could do now as she tilted her head back ready to receive me. Her pussy was wet, swollen, open begging for me to come inside. Taking control she took my dick by the swollen shaft and led the head inside her slowly. As I entered her I felt her go limp in surrender, her legs wrapped around my waist and I could tell it had been awhile since anybody had been inside her tight walls. Thrusting into her aggressively until my balls were pressed into her ass, I began stroking in and out. Out slow and in hard as I thought she could possibly take. Her legs and arms were wrapped around me like I was life and she needed me to sustain herself. She moaned in my ear, and I could tell she was trying to keep her volume down but it was a struggle. That shit made me thrust into her harder, hoping to break through that careful control and make her ass go crazy. But the feel of her tight, wet pussy, clenching around my dick each time I slid in and out was about to push me over the fucking edge.

Soon her moans were getting louder and I wondered if we'd have maintenance up here asking questions. At the same time I didn't give a fuck this shit was intense and the exhibitionist in me almost wanted to give them fuckers a live show. That did something to me and I went into over drive, fucking her until the dam desk was moving across the room.

"Damn baby, don't slow down" Chrissy moaned

"Tell me you want it" I said as I pushed my dick in deeper

"I want it baby" She moaned "I want you to cum with me!"

She wrapped her arms around my neck and began bucking hard as hell. I could tell she was getting closer to cumming. I stroked, she screamed, I stroked harder, she screamed louder, I stroked in hard sliding almost completely out and rammed back in, she completely lost it.

"Shit baby, shit, fuck, I'm cumming" she screamed.

I could feel the tingle in my balls that let me know I was about to cum and she could see the look in my eyes as well.

"Cum for me baby" she cried out "Cum for me"

"Shit" I groaned as I felt us release at the same time. She bit down on my shoulder muffling her cry of pleasure. Her warm wetness and my shot of cream mingling inside her almost made my dick hard again. But Chrissy suddenly collapsed back onto the desk and my dick slid out, sending a shiver up my spine as I stared down at the beautiful woman in front of me, and the mess we'd made on the edge of her desk. I couldn't resist reaching down and rubbing my fingers in the moisture of our combined orgasm that was sliding out of that sexy ass pussy of hers. Chrissy jerked in surprise, and then looked up at me with a smile.

"Damn....that shit was worth the wait. I didn't know I had that much tension built up."

I gave her a cocky smile back, "I did. I've been wanting that ass since day one."

Leaning down I pulled a nipple free and used my teeth to tug at each nipple ring. She arched into it, grabbing the back of my head.

"Shit."

She said suddenly. "What?" I asked, taking my lips off her hard nipple. But my eyes followed hers, we'd wrecked the fuck out of her office...or we'd fucked it into a wreck. Papers were everywhere, her laptop, phone and purse were on the floor and we'd moved the desk clear across the fucking room. I looked down at Chrissy and we both fell out laughing.

"That was some serious shit," I said, pulling her up to a sitting position.

We both laughed again, dressing quickly and attacking the mess we'd made. Just as I was moving the desk back, one of the maintenance ladies walked by and peeked in.

"My God what happened in here?"

We both looked up startled. There were still papers everywhere, we thought we'd move the desk before addressing what fell off of it. Chrissy's hair was tousled in the sexiest, most telling way. Her lipstick was smudged, my shirt was untucked, my tie was across the chair and Chrissy's shoes were still in the corner. There was no denying how it looked was what it was, but we lied anyway.

"I was trying to decide how I wanted to change my office around since I was still here, so I asked if he could stay behind and help" Chrissy said quickly.

"Yeah, I added, big desk you know, heavier than I thought it would be. Had a little spill."

We both glanced quickly at each other and then away, trying to contain our laughs.

With a smirk the maintenance woman replied "Well it looks like you had all the help you needed." As she walked away she added, "Might want to move a little more quietly next time..."

THE CONQUEROR

She strokes me
Provokes me with poking
Hoping no words spoken
Would convey her message
We're progressing
Exposing the thoughts we've been repressing
Feelings we've been suppressing of
Testing the water
The temptation is harder to resist
My mind craves her lips
Hands ready to grip her hips
As we kiss
But we're far from this
Truth is we just met
Don't want to regret our actions
With her there's no acting
My mental is reacting
to her stimulants
The possibilities are limitless
Drawn up several images I'd like to share
Soft strokes of her hair
Seductive glares
Vigorous removal of the clothes we wear
Gasp for air
As our tongues engage each other
We become engulfed in a battle of lovers
Wage war under covers

That protect us
Victory states we can't rush
But we cross boundaries
They said we can't touch
And wage war
But there can only be one Victor
Who wants it most
Her first attempt were close
I was almost subdued
But I had to remember if I'm to lose
I have a point to prove
Before I give in
The goal is me winning
When we switch positions
It's a given
We're both great leaders
But I'm determined to defeat her
She's determined to stop me
The objective is to be on top of me
When she conquers me
Damn I forgot that we just met
But I'm ready for this conquest
Hand to her chest
Fondle breast
Nipple twist
To initiate slight pain
She moans
I twist again
We both know this game well
My dick swells
Her clit gives a show and tell
So I pay attention
then give her all the inches she could take
til she shakes
Uncontrollably
I leave a lasting impression
So she knows it's me
She's holding me
But begging me not to stop

I rest on her spot
Give her constant shots
Til she calls out
Constant back shots til she falls out
Legs sprawled out
She let it all out
Til there's nothing left to give
Her orgasm is the only gift
As I conquer her

THE RUNNERS

The weather man predicted that it was going to be one hot ass day so I figured that I would go out for a morning run on the trail that's close to my house. It was about 5:00am so it was still fairly cool and the sun was just rising. I was very shocked to see someone else there at this time in the a.m. I guess they were thinking the same thing I was about beating the heat and getting the morning run in early. I had been running for about 15 minutes before I got the chance to see the unknown runner that was there with me. As I was running I could see a curvy figure coming towards me. To my surprise the figure got curvier, fuller, and to my surprise more beautiful. I was intrigued even more with what I was seeing. As we passed each other on the trail I couldn't help but think how sexy this woman is. Our eyes locked as we got closer to each other.

"Good morning, great day for a run isn't it" I said with the biggest smile.

"Good morning" she said "It's a great day to be doing a hell of a lot of things.

I have to say that comment caught me off guard as she passed me. But there was so many thoughts that went through my mind so I responded with a hint of cockiness.

"Hell yeah it definitely is" as we both continued on our way.

Like most typical men I couldn't help but to survey what her ass looks like. So I peeked back to see the perfect juicy round ass, not to mention the fact that she wasn't wearing panties either. As I was looking at her, I didn't notice that she was looking back as well getting her eye full of me. Trying to refocus, I turned around to concentrate on the trail ahead, couldn't afford a spill out here. Not a second after that thought, I was alarmed by a scream of pain. Without a second thought I turned around and ran towards the sound, to find my fellow runner sitting on the ground holding her ankle, staring in my direction.

With a slight twinge of guilt I realized I was kind of happy to have the opportunity to talk to her again. I guess it wasn't the most gentlemanly thing given the fact that she was hurt. I knelt to check her out.

"Are you ok," I asked, looking into her big beautiful eyes. I knew my attention should be on her ankle but dam she had a mesmerizing face to go with her sexy, athletic body.

"Damn this shit hurts" she said as she clutched her ankle. "I think I tripped over a rock or something and went freefalling."

"You should have been focused on your surroundings instead of trying to look at my ass, nasty girl." I took her ankle in my hand and flashed her my million dollar smile.

"Ha, Ha, Ha, very funny, but I wasn't the only one staring now was I?"

She was right, I couldn't help but to stare at her. I couldn't understand why she was out here running alone with a body like this. She needed protection out her. From what I saw she had the perfect body. No stomach, toned legs, nice round breast, and a nice firm juicy ass that set up so nice.

"Well I guess that ends my run for the day."

"Would you like me to help you to your car?" I said offering my hand for assistance so she could get up.

"Awe, such a gentleman" she said "I think I'll have to say yes to that offer."

Leaning down I put one arm under her thighs and the other on her back, scooping her up into my arms effortlessly. I could tell she was a little startled but from the look on her face once she was secure in my arms she was enjoying it.

"I'm feeling better already" she said as rested her head on my shoulder.

"Is that so" I said as I pulled her closer into my chest to get a better feel of her.

Her scent was warm and clean. She must have just started her run because she only had a light glaze to her skin. The feel of her body in my arms was so damn intoxicating. She was soft but she also had the toned body of a runner, I could almost feel how agile and limber she was. I couldn't help but to shift my hands slightly to get a better feel of just how soft her ass was.

"Easy tiger, you gotta wait til I say it's ok to touch it" she said jokingly.

Thrown off guard by the fact that she'd caught me I couldn't help but flash an embarrassed smile at her.

"Now you can touch it" she said playfully trying to ease my discomfort.

THE CHALLENGE

Surprising,
No surprise we're here.
This moment we patent moaning without the right to own it.
Opponents with the same intentions we intended for pleasure.
Romantic gestures,
Suggestive suggestions for both of us to follow.
With no thought of tomorrow we wallow in our thoughts.
Desires we fought,
Taught us that mouths closed don't get fed.
Fed our fire with an igniter that ignited these six words.
Can I make love to u?
Words that I'm sure you've heard before.
Defined many ways but my definition means more.
Yes part of it is physical
But I want to make your spiritual scream screams
That make atheist believe in God
Long enough to say God damn to the love we make.
Aware of what's at stake we partake in the forbidden,
Explorers exploring the hidden treasure we've hidden in each
other.
Only thought that keeps me driven is being better than your last.
Lasting long enough to become your last I ask can I make love to
you?
Can I stroke you soft, slow, and steady?
Can I cherish cherished possessions you keep?
Sample fruits forbidden but sweet.
Eat in your garden til your days nutrients deplete.

Can I greet you with the sun rise?
Stare in those beautiful eyes,
Kiss lips that leave drips of ecstasy
I just don't want to make love, I want to give you the best of me,
Suppress cries of desire with what's left in me,
Give affirmation to destiny.
Its destined we partake in our part.
Conquer the heart part before hard parts interfere.
Overcome fears you've feared,
Fear has no right operating here so let me relax you.
Give you something to come back to.
Reactions to react to,
Not because you want to but you have to.
So I ask u.... Can I make love to you?
But not just any type of love we make
I want that kind that makes more than just your hands shake
I'm talking sweat beads to face
remnants of the way you taste
bodies entangled with no space
waist to waist
soft strokes to the face
venturing to that place
where climax
equals combat
but we come back several times
and wage war
We managed to find a common interest worth fight for
When we make love

MEDICAL ATTENTION IS NEEDED

I looked down into her eyes as I stood with her held her cradled in my arms. She looked back at me unabashedly, so I very deliberately shifted her in arms so I was palming her firm ass. Instantly I could feel myself getting hard. I mean what man could resist? Here I am with this sexy ass chocolate woman in my arms who smells absolutely amazing. Unable to control my wayward body parts, I stopped, noticing a picnic table sitting off in the cut. I carried her over to it and sat her on top of the table. I stared into her surprised eyes and then pulled her into a kiss. She responded immediately putting her arms around my neck to pull me deeper into the kiss. The kiss grew more intense as our tongues battled each other. Suddenly I was aware that her legs were open in front of me so I pressed closer in between them. My dick was completely hard now as it rested directly on her throbbing pussy. Her running shorts just couldn't conceal her heat box. I ran my hands down her back still battling with her lips as my hands found her ass on the picnic table and I pulled her in to me. She let out a soft moan as we continued in our tongue war.

I put my hand inside her shorts to feel her soft skin. Damn was it soft!-and so smooth. She felt warm against me as I tightened my grip on her ass. Moaning into my mouth on hers she took put her hands under my shirt and began rubbing her small hands across the planes of my chest. Caressing and exploring me with eager fingers. I was so turned on just letting this random woman learn my body as I explored hers. Taking one hand from her ass, I slid it under her shirt, finding her hard nipples pressed against her sports bra. I immediately rolled one between my thumb and forefinger gently.

"Damn that feels good." She arched her breasts into my hand and leaned up to kiss me again.

"Does it" I asked, continuing my assault on her breasts.

"I think we need to find a more closed off area before we go any further, that is unless you have somewhere else to be right now."

My eyes widened in surprise as she looked at me hopefully.

Somewhere to go! Shit even if I did have somewhere to go I wasn't going to make it. Never in my wildest dreams could I ever imagine being in a situation like this. So the thought of anything else but fucking the shit out of her right this minute was inconceivable.

"Maybe you're right" I said as I stood up, scooped her back up in my arms and began walking a little further onto the path. I walked a ways before noticing another picnic table off under a patch of tree's. You had to duck through the bushes to get through it, so unless someone was on the same shit we were on, we'd be protected from anyone walking up on us. I ducked below the tree's carefully not to injure her in the process. It was almost a perfect circle of tree's in a shaded area. It was small, but just right for what we were trying to do. In fact I absently thought how odd it was that the picnic table was sitting in this small area…maybe someone else had had the same idea as us.

"Perfect," she said, smiling up at me.

I smiled back and then sat her on top of the table, quickly kneeling between her legs. I spread them apart so I could get closer, starting by lifting her thin shirt and kissing her stomach. I spread light kisses over her flat belly, making my way down to her short, fitted running shorts. I inhaled her taking in the sweet smell of her pussy, I was sure she was already wet. Pulling her shorts down gingerly, I exposed her fat pussy lips…no panties, just like I thought.

With her hands on my head I could hear her moan as I continued kissing her. I moved my hands from her thighs up to her pussy. I could feel the pulsating of her clit as I ran my fingers across it several times. Taking my time pulling her shorts off completely I continued kissing her stomach. I could hear her breathing deepen as I finally pulled the shorts off.

"You ok" I asked as I put her legs on my shoulders.

"Is that a trick question" she replied questioningly while attempting to catch her breath.

Before she could say anything else I buried my face between her thighs. She tasted amazing as I drank in the sweet juices her pussy was giving me. I flicked my tongue up and down very light before giving her deep strokes of my tongue-running it across her clit then in and out of her pussy hole. A delved in a little further with each lick, taking brief moments to suck on her clit. I could feel her body go completely limp as she rested on my shoulders.

I looked up to admire the fact that her eyes were shut tight, her head hanging down, her breathing sporadic, then she started moaning, and biting her lip with each stroke of my tongue. I didn't want to stop licking her pussy, flicking my tongue against her clit, and at times sucking the juices from her lips. From this angle I slid my hands up and down her soft legs before I took my fingers and slid them across her swollen lips.

"Damn you're wet as hell" I said with her pussy juices all over my fingers and mouth.

She smiled at me appreciatively before raising a seductive brow in thought.

"Hey, rest on one knee and put the other one up please."

I obliged quickly, kneeling in front of this strange woman like I was proposing with her wetness on my tongue, in my nostrils and on my fingertips. She took her good foot and rested it on my knee, angling her hips so that I had a better angle for tasting her pussy. I took middle and ring finger and slid them across her lips, taking my time sliding them in little by little until my fingers were inside her to the hilt. As I slid them in and out her pussy I took my thumb and circled around her clit to give her deeper stimulation. She started moaning uncontrollably at this point and all her weight was resting on my shoulder and knee. I continued using my fingers to probe her insides as I began sucking her clit, pausing long enough to taste the juices her pussy was releasing. She let out a low groan, signaling to me that she was about to cum. Then she pressed further into my lips until her pussy lips and my lips were fused together. She ground into my tongue and fingers. I started sucking harder, probing deeper, fucking the shit out of her with my hand and mouth, slurping up all she had to give. Her groan turned into a long moan and I knew she was right on the cusp. I licked and sucked as hard as I could.

"FUCK, DAMN BABY, MMMMMMMMMM" she screams "DON'T STOP BABY, PLEASE DON'T STOP, I'M ABOUT TO CUMMMMMMM!"

Like a water slid her wetness rushed out onto my tongue and she collapsed into me. I continued licking and sucking her pussy lightly, letting her catch her breath. After a few minutes of deep breathing and light tremors, she started to regain her composure. Her grip relaxed and she fell back onto the table, giggling softly.

"Damn I needed that" she said taking her legs off of me.

"Well I'm glad I could help you with that" I said, trying not to sound too cocky.

As I stood up, she pulled me by my shirt, bringing my lips to hers. She pushed her tongue into my mouth, seeming to taste her own wetness. It must have been turning her on because she pressed her breasts into me and deepened the kiss further. We were at like we'd known each other forever. I pulled back and pulled my shirt over my head, she mimicked me pulling off her shirt. I leaned over and snatched off her sports bra so I could see those tits that had enticed me as she ran. She sat on the table naked except for her running shoes and socks. Her body was amazing, she had the perfect tits and as I breast man I felt like a kid in the candy store. I was loving that plump ass to. She snapped me back to attention pulling my shorts down over my ass.

"Baby why don't you lay down and let me have a taste of that gorgeous dick of yours."

Without any hesitation I laid back on the table next to her, giving her the chance to please me in return. She took a seat between my legs, running her hands across my belly, kissing my chest softly working her way down to my stomach, leaving a trail of wet kisses. Once she got to my inner thigh were my hard, throbbing dick rested, she took it in her hand and pooped it in her mouth immediately sucking me to the back of her throat. Caught so off guard, I let out a loud moan.

"OOOOOOHHHHHHHH FUCK!"

She looked up at me and smiled, knowing what she was doing to me. Giving me full strokes sucking me in slowly and all the way to the back of her throat. Absently I placed my hand on her head guiding her movements, she chuckled softly, still sucking. Then she reached down to cup my balls with her left hand, giving them a firm squeeze.

Oh shit! I needed a distraction or I was going to bust right in her mouth.

"I want to taste you too" I said.

Without hesitation she positioned herself over my face as she continued deep throating my dick.

I took my fingers and inserted them into her wet throbbing pussy while sucking on her clit. She responded immediately moaning and humming in pleasure as she sucked my dick deep in her mouth. Her pussy was dripping wet so I grabbed her ass cheeks and buried my face in her warm wet insides.

"Damn it woman, you gon make my bust from this" I said before taking her clit in my mouth and sucking harder.

"No baby don't, I need to feel you inside me."

She stopped sucking immediately and lifted herself from my grasp. Shifting around on the table gingerly she straddled me. Holding my dick against her opening she slid slowly onto my dick, taking me all in and her wetness welcomed me, squeezing me tight. Tossing her head back, she closed her eyes and started working her hips on top of me. We were both panting and moaning in unison, I had my hands at her hips guiding her movements, thrusting back into her, as she held onto my chest.

"Shit that feels so fucking good," I said as she slid up and slammed her pussy down on my dick.

She lifted up off my dick only leaving the head inside her pussy, looked down at me and said, "I want you to fuck me from this position." She looked so sexy sitting up over me, my dick just barely inside her.

Anchoring myself onto her hips, I thrust upward hard and pulled back slow. She let out a squeal and braced myself to do it again and again. First slow then fast, deep, deeper, then the deepest to the point where her ass was slapping against my thighs.

"Harder, go harder" she yelled.

I began stroking fast as I possibly could. Hell I thought absently, at this rate I was gonna fuck around and get a splinter stuck in my ass cheek. But she felt so damn good it would be worth it. Reaching up between thrusts I took one of her nipples in my hand and begin squeezing it as she took one hand from chest to start rubbing her clit. Our breathing quickened and our moans seemed to get louder and louder. Each time I stroked inside her she met my dick with a stroke of her own, faster and faster until she climaxed again.

"OOOOOHHHHHHH MMMMMMM IM CUMMING!"

She collapsed on top of me, but I wasn't done. So while she was resting I slid deeper inside her pussy. I couldn't stop now, I was too close to busting myself. Seeing the need in my eyes, she leaned up and started grinding on my dick. This shit was getting so good I can't help but moan. She took her tit and stuffed it in my mouth while bucking her hips hard as hell. I could feel the nut building up inside my balls as she slammed down on my dick and bit into her full breast. Unable to hold back any longer I released inside her. That shit coursed through my entire body as she continued stroking it, trying to get all the nut I had in me out.

She kissed me and giggled, she had to know she'd just fucked the shit out of me. I had to admit this was a first. I had never experienced anything like this and from the looks of it she hadn't either.

"I swear I don't want to get up from here right now," she said.

Shit neither did I but if we didn't I'm pretty sure someone would see us and there would be some questions to answer.

"Me either, fuck," I said as I stroked her back.

She stood up and started getting dressed and I figured it was time for me to do the same thing. As we dressed we couldn't help but to stare at each other and laugh.

"Looks like your ankle is doing much better" I pointed out as she stood on it to put her shorts back on.

She giggled, "Hey I had to do something to get you to stop and come back."

"Is that so?" I said shocked at her comment.

"Don't get me wrong, she said quickly, I've never done anything like this ever…but I have always dreamt of how it would be."

"So how was it" I said with an arrogant smirk on my face.

"Everything I dreamt of and more" she said as she leaned in to kiss me.

Now that we were completely dressed I started walking her back to her car and just like I suspected all the runners were out on the path now. We both laughed and continued our walk. Once we get to her car I told her how much I enjoyed this whole experience. She told me she enjoyed it as well and if it didn't have to end it wouldn't have. We exchanged numbers and parted ways. Once in my car I realized I didn't even know her name so I blew my horn to get her attention before she pulled off. I drove up along the side of her car to find out the million dollar question.

"I never caught your name" I said flashing her an apologetic smile.

"That's because I never gave it" she said with a hint of seductive sarcasm.

"Well I need to know the name of the woman who just fucked the shit out of me" I said

As she shifted her car into drive she smiled and said "Mariah" before pulling off.

SEXPERT

Can u handle tongue tips
soft drips over places that flow freely
Twisted pleasures as teasers
just to elevate you to a place
where displaced faces
would be made easily.
Can u handle light squeezing
of mounds meant only for supplement
designed for succulence
meant to be sucked and licked
to erection.
I'm already erected
but right now it's not about me.
I'm asking for flood gates
to be set free.
Rain down on me
til soaking wet
isn't only a state of being.
I apologize if I'm being to forward
or aggressive
but aggression pinned up
doesn't help either one of us.
I'm trying to make your blood rush

to places that'll cause your head to spin
I believe in repetition
so I prefer doing it over and over again
I desire to see
that smile when you bend.
That grin that speaks volumes
on how you need this.
Let me kiss lips
sip till it drips uncontrollably.
There's no controlling me
so holding me is outta the question.
Handcuffed with your hands up
are required for this session.
1st lesson.....
there's pleasure in undressing.
Teeth removing anything
offering protection
just to see you naked
You get chills
as my tongue taste everything sacred.
2nd lesson....
screaming is accepted.
Tell me "come get it"
help me know whose is it
and when I'm in it
Don't bite your lip when I hit it.
That excites me more.
3rd lesson.....
feet to the floor
arch your back just a little more
never try to keep score
you'll lose count
4th lesson.....
prepare to mount

take in every ounce
till there's no room left
control your breaths
hands to chest
feed me your breast
right to left
till my deepest appreciation
is expressed
5th lesson.....
riding is a blessing
I know you're blessed with
You guessed it
control your pace
let me see the face you make
as you stroke it
soak it till you provoke it to cum
Leave it numb when you're done
But save some for later
I promise the next lesson
will be much more greater......

THE COUGAR

I was alarmed as the bell rung causing my thoughts to go into a panic of sexual frustration, and disbelief from the person waiting on the opposite side of the door. I have been waiting on this all day so to have it coming to pass is well worth the wait. Was I ready? How do I look? What's about to happen? These are the thoughts running through my head as I checked to make sure I was decent. My pajama pants were untied with a black fitted tank top that fit around my body to make sure she could see every muscle, every ab, and every oblique I had.

"What are you doing Anthony?" I said to myself as I walked towards the door.

To be totally honest none of that stuff will even matter seeing that this woman drove all the way here in the middle of the night. She could care less about how I look, that thought at this moment is so unimportant.

As I looked through the peep hole I couldn't help but to get even more excited as I looked at Ashlee waiting on me to answer the door. I turned the lock to unlock the door then reached for the handle to open it still surprised at the fact that she was even here. As I opened it I smiled at her and she returned a very seductive smirk before walking inside. The perfume she had on sent my body through a combination of sexual thoughts and feelings. Her walk told me she was well aware of what she was getting herself into as she surveyed my foyer.

We officially met at a friend's house warming party a few weeks prior but we had seen each other several times in passing around the neighborhood never speaking, never really paying much attention to each other. Well maybe she didn't but I did. I saw her one evening out at my favorite restaurant The Signature Room with what I would later find out was her husband. She was eleven years older than I but looking at her she didn't look a day over thirty. There had always been something about an older woman that intrigued me and everything about her did just that.

While at the house warming party we chatted a little and I found out that we had so much in common. But it wasn't until one of our favorite songs came on that we really broke the ice. You know how it is at most parties when that one song comes on and you have to find the courage to walk up to the most popular girl in the room. Well that was exactly how I was. Scared out of my damn mind but I knew I wanted to dance with her.

"This will be the last song" the DJ spoke over the music as It's Getting Late played through the speakers. That song, the slow mellow song caused every nervous bone in my body to immediately turn into a lustful one.

"Would you like to dance?" I said reaching for her hand.

"I thought you would never ask" she said as she put her hand in mine.

As we danced it seemed like everything and everyone in the room suddenly disappeared and it was just us. I couldn't help but get lost in her until suddenly I felt her hand slide from my shoulder to my chest. The look in her eyes told me where she wanted to go as she whispered in my ear how much she was enjoying this.

Everything about her made me hard as hell and I know she felt the bulge resting on her thigh.

"Looks like someone else is enjoying this just as much as you are" she said sliding her hand down to the throbbing bulge inside my pants.

Surprised by her actions I tried to play it off with a shy grin and apology for what was going on.

"Don't worry, I won't tell if you won't" she whispered in my ear.

That comment made me extremely hard. I didn't want to read too much into her comment so I just continued dancing but as each minute passed I would test the water. First sliding my hands up and down her back until they finally rested firmly on her ass. When she didn't react abruptly I slid them lower til I had a full hand of her soft juicy ass.

"Feels good doesn't it?" she said as she buries her face in my neck and begins giving it soft, light kisses.

"Damn that shit feels good" I said while squeezing her ass harder.

As the song ended for everyone else it was just beginning for us. We never let each other go. We continued dancing as if music was still playing.

"Come on Ashlee" one of her girls yelled from across the room.

"Coming" she yelled back "Oh how I wish I was cumming," she whispered for my hearing only.

GETTING LATE

It's getting late
Well aware of what's at stake
Better yet fate
Can't fake
This feeling
Everything about this moment's
Revealing itself
The desire for you and no one else
Is evident
But I have to be delicate
With what you offer
My touch has to be softer
When your speech begins to falter
More than it's accustomed to
And despite the desire for clutching you
I have to make sure you're comfortable
With everything I want to do
In this moment of time
So I gently trace the design of your spine
Til I find it
That spot you're hiding
The one that's defining
The one that gives your breathing timing
With each second it quickens

I listen
Count the breaths a minute
Before I begin kissing
That feeling of submission takes over you
That's what it's supposed to do
More kissing
Combined with holding you
Exposing you
To feelings unknown to you
I know just what you need
So speed isn't a factor
You need to feel
What comes after this
Ecstasy and pure bliss
Pain with a pleasurable twist
Moans til your mouth submits
To me
Yes we
Are nowhere near done
I want the moon to tell our story to the sun
Tell how we begun
Speak on what was done
And when we're done
We'll let the sun see
Just what happens
When it gets late for you and me
But this was only a level of intimacy
We're entering into
I'm trying to help you forget you
Break down that wall
Of protection
That's protecting
Your erogenous zone
You moan don't
But I won't let up

You pull for me
But I can't get up
Too soon
I want you to travel
Past the four walls of this room
As I consume you
Go ahead and lose you
As I touch the place
Where taste is desired
I'm trying to extinguish that fire
Take your pitch higher
With each lick
Slow yet swift
Soft yet stiff
Just enough to lift you up
I want you to moan
Til you've had enough
Close your legs just enough
To make it hard to breath
Give me what you need
Let me hear you scream
Then cream all over me
Grip while holding me
Escape with the feeling
Til you once again know it's me
That's there
I need to see that stare
That glare of satisfaction
As you try to understand
What happened without asking me
Just know I wanted to give you
A reason to come back to me
It's Getting Late

THE PREY

"Oh how I wish I was cumming" she softly moaned as she let go of me.

We exchanged numbers and made a promise to keep in touch with each other. We spent several week's texting and Facebook messaging each other things that we wanted to do with each other and tonight our conversation went from casual to intense. She began telling me how much she hated sleeping alone because her husband was always out of town on business.

"Well whenever you're free you can come sleep in my bed, or at least attempt to sleep" I said jokingly.

"I just might take you up on that offer" she said in response.

Not thinking too much more into what would actually happen but curious I decided to give her my address. We continued our conversation for about 30 minutes laughing about the things that went on throughout the day and then all of a sudden she went quiet. I figured she had fallen asleep or something…. Until my doorbell rang.

It's now 3am and here in my foyer she stood in a red three quarter length trench with a pair of the sexiest red stilettos on. Still in total disbelief that she was standing here in my place I flashed a smile in her direction.

"What are you doing here?" I said.

"Let's not play coy now. You told me whenever I didn't want to sleep by myself your bed was always available right?" She began unbuttoning her coat as she spoke.

As the last word came out of her mouth she unbuttoned the last button to reveal a black lace bra with a matching lace thong. Her body was amazing. Standing about 5'2 peanut butter skin tone, those breast had to be about a 36 C (I know my breasts), with a tiny waist and the roundest hips to accompany a juicy ass. If this was what she wore to bed I don't understand how she could ever be left alone.

I guess I was lost in my thought too long because before I knew it the coat was on the floor and she was in my arms, kissing me passionately, giving me all the sexual tension and frustration that she apparently was holding in. Her kisses were unlike anything I had ever felt as her tongue began dancing around in my mouth trying to attack my tongue. Our hands lost total control as they began exploring each other's bodies, grabbing, squeezing, touching, and caressing everything we could get our hands on. Damn she felt amazing. It had been a few weeks since I had her in my arms like this, I flashed back to us dancing that night of the housewarming. I never expected to be here with her again but I wouldn't waste a moment, I was going to enjoy this.

With no restraints, no rules, no eyes, no friends, just us, my hands slid up her back to swiftly unstrap her bra.

"MMMMMM" she moaned as I traced the outline of her body's curves. My left hand grabbing her ass, firmly gripping it in my hand wishing that thong was off, pulling her towards me so she could once again feel how hard I was. My right hand stroked her perky, firm breast. Each touch was followed by an even stronger moan as her kisses got even stronger. Her body was damn near trembling in my arms as she sucked my bottom lip. Hoping that she wasn't afraid or regretting what she was doing I pulled back to make sure she was ok.

"OOOOO baby please don't stop" she said before attacking my tongue again.

From that moment forward we were at it. She tore the tank top I had on off and begin kissing and sucking on my chest. I was totally lost in the sensation of her body against mine. She suddenly began slowing stepping back, trying to catch her breath, and smiling hard as hell. The look in her eyes as she stepped told me that I was her prey and she was getting ready to attack me at any moment. But I was determined to get to her before she could get to me so I stepped forward pushing her against the wall so she couldn't step away from me anymore. Once she was on the wall I began a full attack of her body, easing my hand inside her thong I could feel how wet she was.

A long moan left her lips as I ran my fingers across her wet pussy lip.

"MMMMMMMMM BABY" she said reaching for my hand as I started caressing her clit.

She moved my hand so she could slide of her thong quickly. There was no turning back from this now. She looked up at me and the look in her eyes told me to take it.

CLIMAX

Slowly she moves for me
Voice soothing me to relax
She caresses my back
Soft kisses just to see me react
Differently
Tonight she has another entity
In mind
Words become hard to find
Fingers run the design of my spine
As she inches lower
Natural reaction to hold her
But she won't allow me to
She whispers "just lay back"
That's all I'm allowed to do
So I oblige
Never been taken on this ride before
Knees on the floor
She takes it all in
The sensation made it so easy to fall in
Moans and her name's all I'm calling
As she pleases me
She moves so easily
As she eases me in
Treats me like a prize she'll win
If she sees it to the end
But she has other plans for me
She stands for me

Long enough for me to embody her
I get the naughty her
No other eyes ever see
She straddles then rides for me
Moans "are you enjoying being inside of me"
Her screams can't hide from me
With each stroke she releases one
Her speed increases some
She's getting closer
She bites my shoulder as I hold her
She's holding on
Digs her nails in my back
She's holding strong
To the one thing I've been waiting on
I push deeper
The wait is gone
She cums now
Everything she held in comes out
Freely
She continues pleasing
Till I'm pleading for more
Her knees on the bed
My feet on the floor
So I can control her moves
We create the perfect groove
She knew just what to do
To get me there
One hand on her waist
The other in her hair
The journey to ecstasy had begun
We thrust until our battles won
But it gets better
At that very moment we cum together

DEVOURED

Without a second thought I started easing my fingers lower, reaching her wet soft pussy lips, sliding my fingers between them, and feeling the juices that are ready to come out. Ashlee moaned almost uncontrollably as she began shaking against the wall she rested on, while biting her bottom lip. She couldn't help but to grip my wrist as I began playing with her pussy.

"Shit I haven't felt like this in such a long time" she whispered "Please don't stop baby."

I pushed my fingers deeper in her pussy and begin motioning as if I was telling her cum to come down. I could feel her dripping as she started moving her hips, gyrating on my fingers. She positioned herself so I could get a better angle at her g-spot. I could feel her walls pulsating around my fingers as she moans.

"Please fuck me now….yes…. just fuck me baby. I want to feel you inside me."

To hear her begging for my dick turned me on even more. With my free hand I pulled my pajama pants down to reveal my hard dick. Getting a little rougher I quickly turned her around and pressed her up against the wall. Without a second thought she spread her legs and bent enough for her ass to poke out and her face to rest on the wall.

Taking my throbbing hard dick in my hand I guided the head towards her pussy. I inserted it slowly, little by little, so she could feel the pressure. Her pussy was so fucking wet and tight. With each inch I pushed inside she gasped for air. With one deep thrust I was buried inside her. Her pussy walls wrapped around my dick so damn tight, as I began slowly stroking her.

"I'm about to cum for you baby" she said as she began pushing back into each stroke.

Wrapping my hands around her hips I started thrusting my dick in her, harder, faster, fucking her with every ounce of energy I had. She was taking it like a pro, every inch, deep as it could go, screaming she was about to cum. The wetness and slapping noise was driving me crazy as my dick was slamming inside her soaking wet pussy. I could feel her juices all over my dick and feeling how wet my thighs were from her, I was damn sure it was running down her legs. But we didn't stop, we kept going.

"OOOOO that's my fucking spot" she said gripping her ass cheeks, pulling them apart so I could go deeper inside her. Her moaning and screaming was out of control as I licked my thumb and placed it on her asshole, gently teasing it. As I inserted it slightly in her hole I felt her body start to shake uncontrollably again.

"IM ABOUT.....OH MY GOD.....I'M ABOUT TO CUMMMMMMMM!"

I felt her pussy start squirting as she slammed against my dick even harder. I grabbed her hips and started pushing my dick deeper and deeper with each stroke. I wanted to keep her pussy cumming as much as it could.

"Cum for me baby..... I want you to cum inside me....please" she begged.

Before I knew it I felt that tingle in my balls as they slapped against her ass.

"FUCK I'M ABOUT TO BUST" I yelled.

With a few more strokes I found myself cumming hard as hell inside of her wet pussy. I could feel my nut and her cum dripping off my balls. The floor was soaked as I collapsed on her back.

"MMMMMM that's what I've been waiting on. I knew it was worth the wait" she said as she stood up. "Now where's that bed you promised me"

"You ready to go to sleep now" I said as I grabbed her hand and let her down the hall towards the room.

"No I'm ready to fuck you in this bed" she said as she walked past me into the room and laid across the bed.

We fucked in every corner of my house that night. She made sure I knew just where she wanted to be.

THE SUBMISSIVE

She said she was untamable
I told her that depends on who's taming you
I ain't Leo but she know
I walk with a lion's pride
her stride told me she wanted me inside
so I started at the tail
that never fails
the things done there made her yell
swell
in places most would never appease
but that's gold to me
as I sample everything she's showing me
leave a lasting impression so you know it's me
especially when I bite it
you can't hide it
lips begging me to come inside them
just for a taste
slight adjustment of my face
not a moment to waste
I'm all in
king is the only name you calling
Just tell me are you the submissive type
The one that likes to scream and bite
The one who puts up a fight
When he's hitting it right
Do you like whips and chains
pleasurable pain
ties to restrain you
So let's play a game boo

Who comes first
squirt for thirst
tell me it hurts
then ask for more pain
scream my name
It's a game
there can only be one winner
Is it you
Tell me if you're ready to do
everything I'm ready to
If so then it's full steam ahead
Neat and sloppy head
Countertops instead of beds
Ties and restraints for your hands
Ball gags so no words can be said
As you rest in the submissive position
The roughest pleasure is my mission
Tongue twitches
Constant licking
With a deep repetitive flicking
Will carry you into the night
Nipple bites
Hard then light
Put up a fight
Excite me more
More is what you'll beg for
There's more
As I lower you to the ground
You've earned a good pound
So I suggest you bite down
I'm trying to make it hurt
Because what's a full submission
Without a pussy squirt

SECRETS VICI CAN'T HOLD

The past few weeks at work had been intense. We were in the middle of what seemed to be one of the biggest mergers. For the past four hours I had been in my office crunching numbers.

"Damn this shit don't add up" I yelled while slamming the calculator down on the desk.

Suddenly my phone rang and the most soothing voice traveled down the line and to my ears.

"Hey sexy."

It was my Carmen the receptionist calling me.

"Hey" I said still frustrated from the numbers not adding up.

"Oh no, I don't like that tone. What's wrong" she asked with concern in her voice.

"Nothing much, these damn numbers they gave me don't add up and it's frustrating the fuck out of me."

"You are too tense to figure it out right now babe. Stop working for a few and come have lunch with me… My treat."

I really didn't have time to stop right now, I wouldn't be able to focus on anything else until I figured this out…But I didn't want to tell her no.

"Ok I'll meet you at the entrance" I said before hanging up.

Once in car she told me she had an idea. Something that always helped her relax. We listened to music on the radio and jammed to a few cuts that came on. Instead of us going to get food like I thought we were going to do she pulled into a mall. Wondering where her mind was I looked at her and before I could get a word out of my mouth she asked me,

"Have you ever tried twisted retail therapy?"

Unsure of what the hell that was I shook my head no. She turned off the car and we headed inside the mall. I have to admit just the ride alone had taken my mind off work but I was curious as to what the hell this twisted retail therapy was so I played along with her plan. After about 5 minutes of walking and talking we walked over to Victoria's Secret.

"Don't worry, I know how you men are. I won't take long, just need to grab a few things." She said taking my hand and pulling me inside the store.

A store filled with sexy panties, bras, and thongs, what man doesn't love a store like this. What is really going on inside this woman's head I thought to myself? Ain't shit in here for me. She was smiling like a kid in the candy store as she picked up this pair of black panties before making her way over to the bra that matched it. She held them up to her body to get my opinion on them

"So what do you think?" she said dancing with them up against her body.

"They cool" I said trying not to act like imagining her walking around in them wasn't turning me on.

"Boy whatever, don't act like you don't like them." She said as she turned and headed to the dressing room to try them on.

I stood there and watched her switch towards the dressing room curtain before turning and wiggling her finger for me to come with her. Without giving it a second thought I followed her wondering what was about to happen now. I mean me and Carmen just worked together. We never really hung out, just occasionally talked at work. But here I was now following her inside this dressing room.

She walked inside the room and closed the curtain behind her. I stood outside it and waited on her. Catching the eyes of several other women who were in the store shopping for the things they needed I began to feel uncomfortable. I didn't want anyone thinking I was some type of peeping tom or some shit like that. The curtain to her dressing room was cracked open a little and I could see her getting undressed. I watched her slide out of her work clothes and the pair of purple lace panties she had on to try on the black ones she got off the rack. My dick began getting hard as she stepped each foot in and began lifting them up before turning around to watch herself in the mirror. As she pulled them over her firm ass I couldn't help but let out a deep sigh.

She then took off the shirt and bra she had on and tried on the bra that matched the panties.

"Can you help me with this" she yelled to me.

Not sure of what the hell she was on I reached my hands inside the curtain to help her get the bra adjusted the way she wanted it. Before I knew it I was being snatched inside the curtain with her. My eyes were wide open as I looked at her half naked curvaceous body. Perfect breast, slim waist, curvy hips... I got stuck on the black panties that covered her pussy, and looking at her hips I could tell there was definitely a nice ass back there. I could feel myself getting extremely hard now.

She was smiling watching how I was reacting to what I was seeing. I tried my hardest to control that shit but there was no controlling it. I mean everything about her body was enticing. I had so many thoughts running through my head at that moment, how her pussy tasted, what positions could I put her in inside this room, how are we going to do this.

"MMMMM" she moaned as she stared at the bulge inside my pants.

"Carmen what are you doing" I whispered trying not to sound nervous but truth be told, I was.

What the hell would happen if we got caught? I mean we were standing inside a dressing room where anyone on the outside could see us. There was no way in the world we could be quiet inside this little room. Here I was trying to think logically but from the look on her face as she eyed my growing dick I could tell she was like to hell with logic at this moment. As she stepped towards me I tried to take a step back to prepare myself for whatever she had going on inside her head. She seductively looked up at me, placed a finger in her mouth and said,

"Twisted Retail Therapy."

SPEECHLESS

She told me I got her speechless.
She told me how much she needs this.
Told me everything about me
was her weakness
and at this moment
she was her weakest.
This moment in time was designed
for the two of us.
We touched,
just enough
to know what perfection feels like.
Damn she feels right,
and the temptation growing inside me
I could no longer fight.
Tonight would be the night
where we would let go
of every insecurity.
Do things that could be seen
by others as impurities.
Passionate love making
is the only cure I see for my sickness.
No longer wishing for the right moment.
No longer keeping secrets
of the things wanted.
The time is upon us

and we're on it physically.
Her touch does more to me mentally
so the thought of control is nonexistent.
She's persistent to see clay molded,
she whispers she wants to hold it,
begs to let her control it.
Tonight she's her boldest
and with every caress we undress more,
our hand explore
the things we swore to be sacred.
My tongue begins tasting
everything that's naked,
chills lead to shaking,
moans turn to take it,
and with no hesitation I did.
Finally I got a clear understanding
of what perfection is inside of her.
I vibe with her so we match moves,
every thrust she reacts to.
Thinking to myself this has to be mine
as we stare in each other's eyes
and that speaks volumes.
I value every moan she releases,
now her breathing increases
as I go the deepest I'm allowed to.
We lose control
and do the only thing
our bodies know how to
as we softly moan the only word
we know best.
"Yes"

PERECT FIT

Surprised at her response I finally understand what she meant in the car by twisted retail therapy. I tried to contain my composure as I rested on the wall, I couldn't show any signs of timidness, I would have her thinking that I was scared, so I threw all caution in the air. I took her by her waist and began kissing her. Once our lips locked our bodies erupted in a lustful attack, tongues locking into each other, lip biting, no longer worrying about getting caught we were in it. My hands slid into the pair of panties she had on, hands gripping her ass, pulling her to me so she can feel the hard dick that rested inside my pants waiting on her. She pulled off the unlatched bra and let her breast swing freely. Her nipples were hard as hell as I felt them resting on my chest. She then went for my belt, pulling it off quickly before reaching for my zipper. Her movements were swift as hell and before I knew it my pants and boxers were down around my ankles.

Standing there basically naked at this moment we had no care about anything other than what we were doing. She turned to face the mirror, pushed me against the wall and began grinding her ass on my dick. I could feel how wet her pussy was through the panties as she bent over to give me a better angle of her ass. Taking one hand and gripping her waist while taking the other hand and sliding the panties off I could see a swollen pussy ready for me to fuck. As she leaned forward I got down on my knees and began to eat her pussy from the back. I needed to know what she tasted like before my dick got the privilege of feeling her.

"MMMMM" she moaned as she pressed her face against the mirror and arched her back even more so I could get a deeper taste of her.

Flicking my tongue across her clit with her ass all in my face she began grinding my face. I could tell she was really getting into it because my tongue was completely coated with juices from her pussy lips. I took my tongue, inserted it into her and began stroking in and out, slow then fast. She completely lost control from what my tongue was doing to her.

"Fuck me, let me feel your dick inside me, I want to cum all over your dick" she moaned while fucking my face.

I stood up, grabbed the shaft of my dick and inserted the head inside her pussy. I heard her gasp for air as her pussy stretched to allow my dick inside. She slowly pushed deeper with each stroke to try and fit as much of me as she could inside her.

"Damn, that's it" she said as about three quarter of my dick was inside her "I can't take it all baby."

Gripping her hips I pulled her closer to me so she could get the full length of my dick inside her. She damn near collapsed but she took it all in. I began stroking her pussy, hearing the squish sound as my dick slid in and out of her. The only thought in my mind at this moment was how bad I wanted to make her cum. I needed to feel her pussy throbbing against my dick while it was in her.

I gripped her shoulders and pulled her into me even deeper. She began moving back and forward rapidly. She was almost there and to be honest so was I. Doggy style is my favorite positon and a woman that could take my entire dick was an added bonus.

"Cum with me baby" she moaned "you gotta come with me."

The stroking intensified as her walls closed in on my dick. With every stroke inside her I felt myself getting closer and closer to cumming. Finally with one final stroke I felt the hot cum shoot out of my dick inside her waiting pussy.

"MMMMMMM, FFFFFUUUUUUCCCCKKKK" I moaned trying to muffle my groans of release into her back.

"That's what I've been waiting on, now don't you feel better?" she said as I collapsed against the wall trying to regain my composure.

I couldn't help but give her a weak smile. She took all the strength I had left. We got dressed and I quickly slipped out the dressing room and walked towards the counter waiting for her to meet me there. As she approached, she placed the panties and bra that we had just fucked in on the counter.

"I'll take these."

After the cashier rung her up, we walked out the store and headed back to the car. She handed me the bag and smiled.

"These are for you, a reminder every time you're having a rough day all you need is a little twisted retail therapy."

We both laughed and headed back to work. I definitely needed that and I would definitely do more shopping with her in the near future.

SEX EDUCATION

We tied like two ties knotted
plotted our connection
before connecting conversation
prognosis of the situation
stimulating
In more ways than one
raises more than a sunrise
one look in her eyes
was all it took
read like a book
but never turned the page
slaved
by her gaze
amazed
at the way she talked
made sure a lesson was taught
in each session
Sheet wetting 101
deep sweating when that's done
oral testing just for fun
I'm learning
she educates me deeper
anatomy as a teaser
touched on proper procedures
taught me all the features
of the human body

Physical education as a hobby
Fed lunch because I was starving
On to recess
then we rest
time for the next class
basic math
taught me how to add
I'm advanced
So I begin to multiply
learned faster than the other guys
Its rewarding
She smiles then rewards me
nothing about her method was boring
intrigued
Gave my head all it needs
so she stepped back and let me lead
I was well versed
used my mouth like it rehearsed
for the part
I could do this in the dark
blindfolded
Took out my ruler so she could hold it
her apple was golden
given as a token
of appreciation
it was mine
took my time
Reviewed it line by line
made sure our lessons aligned
she listens
her lips made her smile glisten
approval was given
so I continued
made sure to include

things I learned myself
never asked for help
she taught me well
gave me all I needed
I never failed
I excel
She exhaled
had to get her thoughts together
lectured
on my confidence
it's common sense
evident
in her reaction
no need for further action
told her I'd be back when
I need to learn something new
better yet maybe next time
I'll educate you
On what to do
On what I've learned
Give you merits
when rewards are earned
Take turns in role play
Do it day by day
Till you graduate my program
Become a master of no hands
handstands, and back bends
The goal is to make sure
you're never lacking

SEX FARE

Of all the days I picked to work today would be the day. Being the owner of my own limousine company has its perks. I own seven cars and employ 10 drivers. For the most part business runs smooth but lately we have been having problems with one of my VIP clients. She has been complaining about the drivers, saying that they are not fulfilling their duties and she hasn't been pleased. Now this concerned me so I wanted to give her a call to find out what had been going on.

"Good Morning, may I speak to Mrs. Jones?"

"This is she, and it's Ms." said a woman on the other end.

"Oh I'm sorry Ms. Jones this is Mr. Green of Elite Limousine Motor Operators. I'm calling because I got your messages about some issues you were having and I wanted to personally address them myself. What seems to be the problem?"

"Personally address them huh?" she replied seductively.

"Yes ma'am, my job is to make sure that you are pleased and I can keep you as one of my satisfied customers."

"Well to be honest with you the experiences I have had haven't been exactly what I was looking for and I just wasn't satisfied."

"Were the drivers rude? Was their customer service not the best" I asked with concern in my voice.

"No, no, no. It's none of those things. Like I stated earlier, I just wasn't satisfied."

"Well I'll tell you what, I'll be your driver tomorrow. Wherever you want to go, whatever you want to do, I'm at your disposal." I said trying to reassure her that there wouldn't be any more problems.

"Interesting offering." She said "I'll take you up on that, whatever I want right?"

"Yes, whatever you'd like."

We set up a pickup time and location then ended the call. Being an owner of any type of business you have to do whatever it takes to keep your customer happy, to keep their business, even if that means offering your services as their personal chauffeur.

As arranged from our conversation last night I went to pick her up and I must say I was very surprised at who I saw walk out of the house.

"Good morning Ms. Jones" I said as I held the door open for her to get inside the car.

"Samantha will do just fine" she said flashing one of the most beautiful smiles at me. "Yes you will do just fine."

Samantha was every definition of voluptuous. Standing about 5'4 she was the perfect image of a brick house, oh did I forget to mention she was chocolate. Hips, ass, and from the looks of it the nicest pair of juicy breast that set up nicely on her chest. I have never had a thing for chocolate women but she definitely looks like someone I would want to sink my teeth in.

Unsure of what that comment meant we headed on our way to complete the multiple tasks she had planned for the day. From executive meetings, to lunch, to shopping, to another meeting before ending her work day, I have to say this woman was about to wear my ass out. But I didn't let her know that. I had to make sure that she knew how much I wanted to keep her business.

"Anywhere else you'd like me to take you Ms. Jones" I said looking through the rear view mirror.

"Yes now I want to have a little fun. Let's go to the beach."

"The beach it is" I said starting the car.

The weather today was horrible. Ninety degrees with humidity putting it well over one hundred but none of that mattered to her. She was dead set on getting to the beach and having some fun. As we pulled up to the beach I turned to see her in the back trying to put on sunscreen. The way she slid the straps of her dress down while looking at me in the mirror told me that this was going to be more than a beach trip.

"Do you need some help with that?" I asked trying to test the waters.

"I thought you'd never ask," she said.

Surprised by her response, I quickly exited the vehicle and made my way to the back to help her.

"You know you can let your dress down a little more right? The windows are tinted and there isn't anyone in sight, I'm confident no one will see you."

She had no problem doing just that as she had me unzip the back of the dress and completely let it fall. She smiled and I knew she could see the lust in my eyes as I gazed at her completely naked. This whole this woman didn't have any damn underwear on. My jaw was on the floor, the only words I could articulate were,

"Damn."

She laid down on the seat. I slowly rubbed sunscreen on her stomach, arms, and legs. Her eyes closed and she bit her lip, a telling sign that she was enjoying every moment of this.

"MMMM, someone is good with their hands I see."

That ain't the half of it, I thought with a grin. She had no idea what I wanted to do to her at that very moment. I was literally fighting to keep my composure and my dick as calm as possible until....

"Hey you forgot about my breasts" she said as turned to offer them up to me. That alone sent me into what I call "charged status". The sight of her breasts were beautiful. She had to be at least a 36 DD or better, but they set up so perky, so full, with the most swollen nipples I ever wanted to put my mouth on. As I put sun screen on her breast she began to lick her lips and put on a show for me as she took her hand and trailed it down her stomach and in between her legs.

"MMMMM see what you did" she said showing me wet fingers. She licked the wetness off her pointer finger delicately and then stuck two fingers inside herself, grinding her hips into her own hand and moaning. Leaning back into the seats she spread her legs wide and fingered herself with increasing intensity, moaning louder and louder until I was hard as a fucking rock watching her. I'm so glad I picked a spot where it doesn't get too much traffic because at this rate there definitely would be someone listening in at what was going on. All I could do is watch in awe as this beautiful woman, finger fucked herself to submission.

"Oooooh Shit!" she moaned as I watched her whole body with her orgasm. "Fuuuuuuccckkkk," she cried out.

By this point I was breathing as heavy as she was. I wanted to feel her, I wanted to join her as she moaned. Those moans should be caused from me and not her fingers I quietly thought to myself. Seeing that I was in deep thought she took her cum soaked fingers and placed them on my lips, I quickly licked and sucked her fingertips clean.

"I figured you wanted to know what I tasted like" she said as she swirled her fingers around in my mouth.

I greedily sucked the juices from her fingers.

"Mmmmm just as I expected, so fucking sweet."

She stared at my hard, throbbing dick before damn near ripping my pants off me. Once she got my dick out my pants and boxers without any hesitation she pulled me to her and shoved it inside her. She went at it aggressive as hell. The pounding of my dick inside her had me moaning

"Damn baby ple…."

But she couldn't finish her words before my dick was back in her deeper. I was determined to see how many times I could make her cum. I wasn't going to stop until she was dripping all over me. She was taking it like a champ, grinding hard as hell each time I stroked inside her.

Nails dug into my back she screamed "Ooooohhhh go deeper!"

At the rate we were going I knew I would be busting soon. So I quickly flipped her over so I could fuck her doggy style. That has always been my favorite position to be in but from the looks of it that's hers as well and she pushed her face into the seat.

"Tell me how this dick feel" I said grabbing the back of her neck. "Let me hear you say it!" I thrust my dick in her deeper.

"It feels ggggoooooooddddd" she moaned into the seat. "I'M CUMMING BABY, OOOOOOHHHH SHIT I'M

CUMMING."

She reached back and grabbed her ass cheeks while I was slamming my dick inside her. That shit made me lose control.

I grabbed her hips as she slid off the seat to the floor for me to get a better angle and view of her ass bouncing on my dick.

"Cum for me, I need to feel that dick cumming inside my pussy" she moaned.

I began pounding her pussy, faster and faster. This shit was so damn good. We totally forgot the fact that we were in a car and anyone could be walking by at any point. She reached under us, grabbed my balls and began rolling them in her hand as I fucked her.

"Oooh I feel that dick about to cum," she screamed as she felt my dick swell up.

I couldn't fight it any longer as I bust inside her. Her pussy gripped my dick as I shot load after load of cum into her. We collapsed on the floor reeling from everything that just happened.

"So Ms. Jones have I satisfied your request" I said trying to sound as professional as possible.

"You definitely have" she said "I will definitely be using you again very soon."

A LESSON IN SEXING

Slowly she moves for me
Voice soothing me to relax
She caresses my back
Soft kisses just to see me react
Differently
Tonight she has another entity
In mind
Words become hard to find
Fingers run the design of my spine
As she inches lower
Natural reaction to hold her
But she won't allow me to
She whispers "just lay back"
That's all I'm allowed to do
So I oblige
Never been taken on this ride before
Knees on the floor
She takes it all in
The sensation made it so easy to fall in
Moans and her name's all I'm calling
As she pleases me
She moves so easily
As she eases me in
Treats me like a prize she'll win
If she sees it to the end
But she has other plans for me
She stands for me

Long enough for me to embody her
I get the naughty her
No other eyes ever see
She straddles then rides for me
Moans "are you enjoying being inside of me"
Her screams can't hide from me
With each stroke she releases one
Her speed increases some
She's getting closer
She bites my shoulder as I hold her
She's holding on
Digs her nails in my back
She's holding strong
To the one thing I've been waiting on
I push deeper
The wait is gone
She cums now
Everything she held in comes out
Freely
She continues pleasing
Till I'm pleading for more
Her knees on the bed
My feet on the floor
So I can control her moves
We create the perfect groove
She knew just what to do
To get me there
One hand on her waist
The other in her hair
The journey to ecstasy had begun
We thrust until our battles won
But it gets better
At that very moment we climax together

BONDAGE

Bree sat at her desk rubbing her achy feet. It had been a long day of teaching and she was exhausted, too exhausted to get up from her desk and head for the car. Besides she needed to get her mind together for the little stop she had to make on the way home. Smiling ruefully to herself, she thought about how much that release was needed.

Mozart was still echoing softly throughout her small history classroom. Probably the only people left in the school on a Friday night at 10:00p.m. Were her and the custodians. Bree sat and swayed lightly to Moonlight Sonata as it strained softly through her desk speakers, when there was a light knock on the door. Opening her eyes slowly, Bree locked eyes with Myles the security guard for the west end of the school. Straightening up and sliding her pumps back on Bree gave Myles a cool, polite smile. He was a bit of a playboy, and was tossing Bree a cocky smile that said exactly that.

"I heard the music Mrs. Ward, I just wanted to check and make sure that you were alright back here."

Bree looked him over, his statement seemed sincere enough, so she figured she'd be nice.

"That's very kind of you Myles, I'm fine, just working up the energy to head out. We just finished up the fall play and I wanted to tidy up a bit before leaving for the weekend."

"I saw the play Mrs. Ward, your kids did a great job."

Bree smiled broadly, the kids were her soft spot. "They did didn't they? Thanks."

There was a slight pause in the conversation. Myles was steeling himself to make his move, he didn't know how she'd react so he wanted to play it just right. Everyone loved Mrs. Ward's fine ass. Some had tried, but he wanted to be the nigga that succeeded.

Without another thought he said, "I know where all the cameras are in the building."

"Pardon me," Bree responded puzzled.

Myles started walking over to where she stood next to her desk.

"I know where all the cameras are in the building, most think we have them in the classrooms as well as the halls, but we don't. In the at the west end there are even less, in fact, there are none in front of your classroom because it's at the end hall."

Myles stopped arm's length away from Bree. She was looking at him with the blankest expression, head cocked to the side.

"And you're telling me this because..."

"Cause I want you. Now. On this desk, or up against that wall, your choice."

He aimed determined green eyes at her and before he could blink Bree's hand smashed against his cheek. Whipping his head to the side. Without thinking Myles grabbed her arms roughly bringing her to eye level with him. But he quickly released her and stepped back as her soft features hardened into a cruel expression.

Shit...Myles thought, perhaps he'd overplayed his hand. She'd never been blatantly flirty, but her eyes, her body language had always told him a different story...or so he thought. Fuck, fuck, fuck...he could get fired for this.

Quickly he apologized, "I'm sorry Mrs. Ward, I-"

"It's Ms. Not Mrs." Her arms were crossed in front of her and she was still giving him that hard glare.

He looked up at her, shocked that she'd chosen to point that out at this moment.

"I'm really, really sorry, I thought I saw....never mind, I'll go. Please don't report this shit, I'm really-I'm an ass. I'm sorry."

"Dam straight," she finally responded.

Myles quickly turned around and headed for the door, not seeing Bree's hard expression soften into a sensual smirk. It seemed that Myles could take a hit...the stinging in her palm felt so fucking good, and the way he grabbed her. Her gaze traveled down to his tight sexy ass in that blue uniform. Bree didn't usually fuck her colleagues, in fact this would be a first...but lately her sub had started to bore her and she was looking for a new fuck anyway...why not. Top Flight just might have some go. Straightening from her perch on the edge of the desk, she called to him before he walked out.

"Stop."

Myles stopped and turned to look at her. Bree put one hand on her hip, toying with her necklace with the other and assessed Myles with an appreciative gaze. He was medium height, the blue uniform hid what looked like a muscular upper body and a definite print in those blue slacks. His dreadlocks were pulled back into a low ponytail, but she knew they hit him about mid back. A full beard framed, nice lips, especially that bottom one...she wouldn't mind biting that shit, Bree thought mildly.

"Close the door," she said softly, still looking Myles over.

"I'm sorry," Myles said, blinking rapidly.

"Come in, and close the fucking door."

Myles eyes widened, shit! What was this bitch about to do? Without thinking he pulled the door closed and watched her as she pulled down both shades on the windows. Dam, she was sexy as fuck. Myles dick twitched in his pants and he bit his lip admiring her round ass, the kind that a nigga could get lost in. He was part nervous and part excited watching her move around the room. Pulling her large, rolling desk chair over to the corner next to window, Bree motioned him over. Myles walked over slowly and didn't dare breath in the process. Once he was closer Bree, grabbed him by his standard security tie and pulled him to her lips, forcing his head to hers with her free hand. She invaded his mouth with an agile tongue, licking and sucking his lips, then biting and pulling at his bottom lip fiercely. Myles stepped back, momentarily surprised.

Bree laughed soft and low. "I'm about to tear that ass up. You are my bitch now. Sit the fuck down."

Myles froze...could it be possible that sexy Ms. Ward was a dominatrix?

Suddenly Bree aggressively grabbed Myles by his package, massaging it with just the right amount of pressure, while looking him dead in the eyes. She turned her head to the side in wonderment. Mrs. Ballard had been right, Myles did have grey eyes, but you had to be close to tell. Hot...

"Listen sugar, if you want this pussy, you are going to have to learn to fucking follow directions. Now, sit. Your. Ass. Down."

She released his dick and stepped back. Myles absently thought as he sat that he'd never heard little Miss Priss curse before. The shit was sexy as hell. It was in sharp contrast to her usual prim and proper demeanor.

"Good boy," she said as he sat.

Myles looked up at her with curious eyes as she removed her pumps again and walked over to grab her purse. She flipped off the lights and only left her desk lamp on, so he couldn't quite see what she had in her hands.

Adjusting the light, she shined it towards him, so he was momentarily blinded. Before his eyes could adjust Bree was straddling him, pulling his hands behind the chair.

"What the fuck?"

"Don't resist, Bree responded quickly, he could feel her breath on his neck. We're going to have a little bit of fun. You just have to do as I say." She completed her sentence by running her tongue up his neck and to his earlobe, pulling it into her mouth and sucking lightly, before biting down hard.

"Ow, shit!" Myles had never been so confused and turned on. Somehow while she was toying with his ear, he'd been handcuffed.

"Just go with it. You said it was my choice." Bree smiled at him seductively grinding her hips into his growing erection.

Myles could feel the heat from her pussy through his pants and her panties. He let out a groan as he watched her hips rotating on top of him, skirt hiked up around her waist and that beautiful brown skin was exposed. Fuck, he wanted to grab those hips and shove his dick into her warmth, but his dam hands were literally tied...or cuffed from what it felt like. Leaning her breast into his muscular chest, Bree began unbuttoning his shirt and tie, until it hung open. Bree ran her hands down his chest, over his hard abs and started loosening his belt and pants.

"Let's see what you got for me."

Reaching into his boxers she pulled his throbbing dick out and looked down with a smile.

"I can work with that."

Myles gave her a smug smile, "Wait till he's all the way up baby."

Bree took one manicured hand from his dick, reared back and smacked him across the face.

Then leaning in she grabbed his jaw pulling his face to hers. She kissed him hard, wet and long before pulling back and looking at him again.

"Did I tell you to speak bitch?"

She let go of his face roughly and Myles dropped his head, looking at his growing erection. Who the fuck knew he liked rough shit. Somehow that smack had sent a direct message to his dick to get ready. His jaw stung a bit but nothing unbearable.

"Good boy."

Bree climbed off his lap, and Myles head jerked up. She turned around and slid off her skirt, standing in front of him in just a camisole and her very lacy...thong underwear. With a seductive smile, she slowly pulled off her thong and sat on the edge of her desk, facing him with her legs wide. The lips of her pussy were begging to meet his lips. She was trimmed and neat with the sexiest thighs... shit Myles thought. He almost asked to put his lips there, but his cheek had just stopped stinging and he didn't want to chance it. Slowly as if reading his thoughts, she rubbed her hands up and down her thighs, lightly caressing herself, then she reached behind her pulling something small out of her purse.

Myles watched as she moved her hands down to her clit, circling it. Then a small humming noise began as she arched her back into the movement of her hand. Reaching up to grab her own nipple with the other. Myles lips parted in wonderment...he'd had a lot of fantasies about Bree, but shit!

Bree was circling her hips on the desk, enjoying the feel of the vibrating ring and the anticipation building in her at what she was about to do next. She got herself to the brink of orgasm and was going to stop there but thought, to hell with it might as well come. Shoving two of her own fingers inside of herself, while keeping the ring at her clit, Bree squirted hot liquid all over her hand, head thrown back in abandonment, moaning softly in release. Sliding the ring off her now lubricated pussy, Bree pushed herself up off the desk and walked towards Myles. Staring him right in the eyes she licked the two fingers she'd used to push her to orgasm. He watched eyes wide, dick growing harder as her titties bounced lightly with each step. She was driving him nuts and he was starting to wonder if she was gonna actually let him in that pretty little pussy of hers.

Stopping in front of him, as if she'd read his thoughts, Bree asked, "So you still want me Mr. Security Guard?"

"Hell yeah," Myles responded quickly licking his lips.

Taking a ruler from behind her back Bree rapped him on his stomach lightly, "When I ask you something you say YES MA'AM."

"Yes ma'am," Myles responded quickly, intrigued by her beautiful crazy ass, sexy as hell in the desk light that was almost acting as a spotlight, highlighting her shape.

Leaning down Bree ran her hand up and down his dick slowly, before pulling a condom out of her bra and rolling it expertly over his penis. Shit, why the fuck was she so prepared? Myles thought absently. Then he jerked in surprise as she slid the vibrating ring she'd been masturbating with over his penis.

"You'll like it. Trust me." She said it in a matter of fact way then leaned down and kissed the tip of his penis.

Myles felt a shiver go up his spine and his dick tingled where her lips had been. This shit was kinky as hell, he was hoping she'd just go head and deep throat the dick. Squatting down in front him Bree lowered the chair until he was eye level with her stomach, he hadn't realized he'd been sitting up so high until she lowered it.

"I think you've seen enough." With that she pulled his tie, dangling loose around his neck and covered his eyes.

"Shit! Wait a minutes!"

The hits came from nowhere and everywhere, the ruler smacked against his abdomen, chest and inner thigh in rapid succession, and then he felt the warmth of her ass against his mouth. Without thinking he bit into her juicy ass, licking her ass cheek like he wanted to lick that juicy ass pussy.

"Oh, you like to be a bad boy huh?"

Adjusting herself, Bree moved her asshole right against his lips, just to see if he'd repeat what he'd done to her cheek. Myles only hesitated briefly before licking his tongue up her crack and into her quickly, exploring her insides with long deep strokes. Bree moaned in pleasure.

"MMMMmmm....she almost hummed, I like that shit, you nasty mutha fucka."

Suddenly she was gone from his face, and there was vibrating at the base of his penis. Before Myles could adjust to the sensation Bree shoved him roughly inside her, sitting on his dick, enjoying the full feeling. Dam this mother fucker was big...she could feel him at the very back of her even in this position. Her ass pressed against his warm, hard stomach and the vibrating ring was positioned right on her clit. Bree just sat a minute enjoying the feeling, knowing she was driving him crazy. When he suddenly tried to move inside her, Bree rapped his inner thigh with the ruler 3 times.

"I run this shit. Don't move unless I say so."

She clenched her walls around him and was rewarded with a loud moan as Myles tossed his head back against the chair in sweet agony. Smiling to herself, Bree rested her hands on the arms of the chair and started circling her hips slowly. Then she added an up and down motion. Circle, circle, up, down, circle, circle, up-circle down, up-down, circle, circle until Myles was panting with the effort not match her movements. Suddenly Bree tightened around him,

"Oh shit," she whispered and squirted all over his dick, leaving a wet mess on his pants.

Finally Myles couldn't take it any longer and he began to move inside her, thrusting up a bit awkwardly at first with his hands behind his back, before finding his pace. This time Bree didn't stop him, she leaned forward grabbing her ankles, sticking her ass farther into his chest and bouncing back on his hard dick, while the vibrator hit her pussy so dam sweetly.

"Oh fuck, Oh..." Bree climaxed again.

Damnit she was a serious squirter and that shit was turning Myles on. The blindfold had him feeling every sensation magnified. The feel of her lush ass bouncing against his belly, the tight, wetness of her pussy on his hard dick, the vibration that was touching something deep inside him and making him hard as hell. Got dam! Bree came a third time before standing up quickly, leaving Myles shaking with the desire to cum already!

He looked around blindly, only seeing the black of the tie around his eyes and faint light around the edges. Suddenly he was sliding into something warm, slick and tight, in and out, in and out. Bree smiled up at him, relishing the fact that he couldn't see her, on her knees in front him, letting him titty fuck her right in her dam classroom. Just to add on to the sensation, Bree leaned down and took the tip of him inside her mouth, each time he slid through her ample breasts she sucked the tip of his penis into her mouth, squeezing her breasts together for added pleasure.

He was slowly beginning to realize what she was doing and he felt himself so close to busting, but he wanted to cum off that pussy, so he tried to hold back pumping up vigorously into her waiting cleavage and hot mouth. Suddenly she was gone again and Myles felt her palm sharp across his face. It barely hurt anymore. Ripping off the blindfold and stepping back, Bree pulled off her camisole and bra. Myles looked up in awe. Her nipples were dark and suck able, he wanted to eat the shit out of her titties and to top it off...she had a small ring in each nipple. She must wear pads in her bra or something to hide it because he definitely would have noticed this shit before! Bree walked up closer, letting him see her titties jiggle as she walked, before sitting straddling him again, this time face forward.

"Hungry?" She asked with a smirk. Before taking one full breast, bending her head down and popping it in her own mouth, sucking and then lightly tugging on the nipple ring with her teeth.

Myles was experiences too many shocks tonight, got dam. His penis was between them, harder than super man's knee cap.

"Ma'am?" He finally squeaked out.

"Yes bitch?"

Myles never had anybody call him a bitch, that shit was fighting words and she'd said it several times. But if her calling him "Bitch" was going to get him that hot pussy he'd take it.

"Feed me please."

With a smile, Bree fed her breasts into his mouth and Myles let her see what his lips could do, biting, teasing, nibbling at her sensitive nipples. Bree kept grinding her hips into him, while her hand stroked his dick up and down. She moaned as he tugged at her nipple ring, wondering distantly how his tongue would feel on her pussy. Quickly Bree switched hands, giving him her other titties while her free hand worked his slick dick.

Finally Bree reached around and un-cuffed him.

Immediately Myles hands came up to grab those luscious breasts in his hands to suck and nibble on them, until Bree's head was tossed back in ecstasy. Lifting up on his lap, she guided him into her and they both started moving completely in sink. Myles thought he'd pay her back for all the rough shit, so moving one hand from her hips he reached to wrap his hand around her throat, Bree looked down at him, " That's right, fuck me."

He tightened his hand around her throat pushing her back so that her body was arched back into the air and he had better access to her tight pussy. With his other hand he started pulling at that sexy as nipple ring again while he ground into her like wanted to tear a whole through her body.

Bree was enjoying the choking shit, but to remind him who was in charge, she reached forward, pinched his nipple, then gave him a hard smack. Myles barely flinched, but tightened his grip around her throat and ground into her harder, feeling his climax approaching.

"That's right, cum for me!" Bree squeaked out, as his hand tightened involuntarily on her throat.

The pressure pushed her to climax, back arched into the air dangerously by his muscular arm. The tightening of her pussy walls and the wet flood on his pants sent Myles over the edge, convulsing so hard he thought his fucking head was going to burst as he spewed hot semen inside her...inside the condom.

"Fuck!" Myles groaned in release.

Finally he relaxed his grip on her throat and she let go of his arm, as she leaned back into his chest panting.

Suddenly Bree looked down in surprise, "what the fuck." Looking back up into Myles grey eyes. He was smiling and already, ready to go again.

"You tapping out Ma'am?"

Bree smiled, getting up carefully, watching the used condom slide out and his amazingly hard dick. Bree leaned down, pulled off the condom and gently pulled off the vibrating ring, while Myles watched.

Straightening up, she said, "Not even."

Standing up quickly Myles flipped her around so that she was facing the wall. Bree directed him to get a condom off the desk, sliding it on quickly, he reared back and smacked her ass cheek, hard.

Bree moaned with pleasure and leaned against the wall arching her back for easier access. Myles smacked her ass over and over loving the feel of it and the way it bounced back at him jiggling and giving him peeks of that moist pussy, unable to stand it anymore he shoved himself inside her again, taking his thumb and placing it in her ass he pounded into her, while she held up the wall moaning wildly and bouncing back into him just as vigorously.

It wasn't long before she let out a little shriek, Cumming hot and wet. Myles loved the fact that she kept that fucking back arched, even when she was Cumming. Smacking her ass again Myles kept pumping into her, knowing he wouldn't last long this time. He felt like a fucking mad man as he rammed into that pussy and her ass just kept bouncing back. Bree reached down to put one hand on her clit pressing down, while keeping the other hand up to protect her head from smashing into the wall. She was slowly losing her mind feeling his thumb in her ass, his dick filling her up and now the pressure she was putting on her own clit, she was about to come undone.

"Oh fuck, oh fuck." Myles suddenly said.

"Oh Shit." Bree moaned into the wall as they both climaxed in almost perfect unison, loudly and wet.

Myles body sagged into Bree and she leaned into the wall, letting her clit go to hold herself up. She was racked with aftershocks, shaking and shivering, while Myles just sat inside her, enjoying the convulsions and having a few of his own. Finally he stood up and pulled out slowly, straightening, Bree turned around to look at him.

They just stood looking at one another momentarily before Bree walked up pressed her tits against his chest and leaned up to kiss him wetly, Myles wrapped her in his arms, palming his ass as she pulled his dreads into her fist, yanking hard and grinding into him.

Suddenly she stepped back out of his embrace and smacked him lightly this time.

"Now get the fuck out my office you nasty bastard."

WHO CUMS BEFORE THE SUN

Honestly
It's the honesty
that moved me to write this
Can no longer fight this
when we kiss I get butterflies
utter lines
that speak of desire
desired you before the fire was lit
you are more than equipped for this
this is more than child's play
so I couldn't act in a child's way
when it comes to you
I come for you
in more ways than one
if you ever wondered what comes before the sun
I'll show you
took the time to know you
so you need not wonder
what we have can't be put asunder
our connection goes way past under sheets
yet in those sheets we'd meet on many occasions
allow misbehaving relations
to get the best of us
no need to rush
as we touch on secret topics
nothing to stop it
we release our thoughts
the things we fought to get here
its here were we can undress
confess, then allow our bodies the sweet rest
leave sheets wet

from what we share
it's because you're here
that I'm wide open
I've listened to the words spoken
and I'm hoping for more of you
you have no idea what's in store for you
before the days done
I'll show you who comes before the sun
so save one
I know you gave one
but there's more to give
let your thoughts live free
just live with me
like that's all that mattered
let our bodies make up the only matter that matters
at this moment
allow our moaning to be the only opponents
we'd face
as we face the only place that looks familiar
peculiar isn't it
as you notice the differences of each stroke
yes these strokes
are meant to provoke things hidden
free that timid timidness before we finish this
trust the finishing
is much better than the start
I wrote the scene
just play the part
let the dark set the mood
as we role play
I want you to hold clay
then mold clay as you see fit
stroke it
while holding it like it's yours
that's what it's made for
give more
til there was nothing left there
just share in this moment
with me moaning in unison

we view the sun rise
as our morning dew slides down
God is the only name we call out
as we let go
We let the world know
what we've done
I told you
I'll show you how it's done
I told you
I'll show you who comes
before the sun
Now come get it!!!!

LETTER FROM THE AUTHOR

Before I say anything else I first want to say Thank You. This has truly been a journey for me. When I first started writing this book I have to be totally honest, I wondered how people would look at me. Would they see me as a freak or pervert? It honestly wasn't until those people I mentioned in the acknowledgements gave me the courage to step out and do it. In this first book I have learned that you can't put yourself in a box as a writer. You have been blessed with a gift and regardless of the content you use it in, it's still your gift.

The Knaughty Poet is the alter ego of Love Personified, and Love Personified is the alter ego of me. Growing up I wasn't one of the kids that most people ever really paid attention to. I was quiet, shy, and extremely different, but even then I was creating characters that would later be revealed. As I got older I found a passion for writing. It wasn't until May of 2008 that I fell head over heels in love with it. That's where Love Personified was created. When anyone asked who that was people would respond "oh that's the guy that walks around counting eyelashes" It's funny as I sit here and think about it now.

But I still felt boxed in, like there was something I was still missing. It didn't become apparent until I went to an erotic poetry show that I found out that there was a place for some of the thoughts I was having. Since that day I started writing passionate erotic pieces. I would try them out at any open mic I could get to and the reaction of people made me want to pursue it further. So my other alter ego was formed.

I was always told that my gift would make room for me and I can honestly say that it has. In this book I found out that I can push the limits, test the waters, and try something different. I am proud of what I have accomplished. I am proud of the person that I have become. This is my passion, this is my motivation, this is what I wake up and see each and every morning I open my eyes. I'm not afraid to acknowledge that this gift was given to me by God. Regardless of the content it's because of him that I have this will to want to write.

I hope that you found something that sparked an interest in you. I can't begin to tell you what it took to finally get to this page. The weeks without sleep, the frustration of writers block, the deadlines, and everything that comes with writing a book. But to be totally honest with you, I wouldn't trade this for anything in the world. For me this is the best part of waking up and it is with great pride that I say that this is........

The End

Or is it.....

Snippet from Fifty Shades of Dark Chocolate.....

Alexis struggled and strained in an attempt to free herself from the bonds that were holding her upright, but despite her many attempts prior to this she was still very unsuccessful. She could feel the black ball gag that was placed in her mouth. There was something about feeling and being helpless that turned her on. She smiled as she thought about that fact that less than 6 hours prior she was sitting at home in her bed, scrolling through her emails when a message popped up across her screen.

Are you bored with who you're fucking? Does that toy still leave you unsatisfied?

She was just about to close the screen out thinking that it had to be some type of pop up until…

Alex cum Join Me

Startled that whoever sent that knew who she was, she clicked to respond and it took her to a blue screen with a hyperlink of five words sitting in the middle that read;

Fifty Shades of Dark Chocolate

When she clicked that an address and time flashed at the bottom of her screen. She was very intrigued to find out who the hell would send her a message like that. Everything in her conscious told her to ignore it, but there was something about those questions that made her get dressed and go to the address to find out what it was all about.

As she arrived at the address she was surprised to see what looked like a normal chocolate colored two story home. She parked, checked out her makeup in the mirror, got out the car and proceeded to the door. Her heart was beating hard as hell as the door opened and a woman greeted her.

"Hey Alexis we've been expecting you," the woman said signaling her to come in.

"I was told to come to this address, and who is we?" Alexis said a little worried

The woman walked to the desk, grabbed a clip board and pen then handed it to Alexis.

"You'll soon find out, but first I need you to fill out this paperwork and bring it to me when you're done," the woman said as she walked backed to the desk and sat down.

Alexis skimmed through the packet of paperwork that she was given and was utterly shocked because almost every page was a nondisclosure agreement but it had her name and a different gentleman's name on it as well. Her mind was working a thousand miles an hour trying to figure out who and where all this came from, but without much hesitation she signed each one and handed the packet back to the woman at the desk.

The woman glanced over the paperwork, smiled at Alexis and tapped the bell that was sitting on top of her desk.

"Someone will be here in a few to get you, she said with the biggest smile on her face, Enjoy."

Unsure of how to really take that gesture and response. Alexis took a seat closest to the door just in case she needed to make a quick dash for the door. About two minutes later two dark skinned brothers in black suits entered the room.

"Alexis" one said

"That's me" she said standing up.

"Come with us" he said reaching for her hand.

They walked in a door that was off in the corner and before she could get a good look at where she was one of the guys stood in front of her.

"I'm sorry but we have to blindfold you" he said pulling the blindfold out of his pocket

"Blindfold me?" she said nervous about what was going on.

"Did you not read the packet? Are we not following rules already Alexis" he said.

Remembering that she did read that in the packet she signed Alexis nodded her head, telling them that she understood. After she was blindfolded the gentlemen guided her to room which sounded like it was empty from the echoes of their conversations. They started carefully taking off her clothes til she was standing there completely naked.

"Open your mouth," said one of the gentlemen.

As she opened her mouth the guy put a black ball gag in her mouth. The other one placed these leather and metal shackles on her hands and feet. The ones on her hands were then secured to a chain that was hanging from the ceiling.

What they needed to do was done as they made their way to the exit, closing the door behind them. Alexis couldn't move at all. She was slightly terrified as to what was about to happen to her but part of her was sexually aroused and curious as to what she signed up for. All of a sudden she heard a door open and the sound of someone walking towards her. Unable to see who it was she was helpless to whatever they had planned for her. She felt the smooth hands of someone caressing her breast and fondling her pussy lips and the dick of another person on her ass.

"Do you want to cum?" said the person that was standing in front of her.

She tried to squeak out "yes" around the ball gag, but settle for nodding instead.

She then felt a hard slap to her ass as the gentleman behind her responded "good girl."

The man standing in front of her began fingering her pussy. She moaned as his fingers stroked in and out of her. She ground her hips against his hand, trying to push his fingers in as deep as she possibly could before she came, but he wouldn't allow her to.

"I didn't tell you that you could cum yet, did I," he asked roughly as he began squeezing her nipple.

She moaned and shook her head no in defeated response

He got down on his knees, lifted her legs up on his shoulders, and began to lick her throbbing pussy. His licks were constant with a light amount of pressure to her clit. She couldn't resist wrapping her legs around his neck.

"You can cum now," said the gentleman standing behind her as he firmly gripped her nipples and gave them a slight twist.

With one last flick of his tongue she experienced one of the most amazing orgasms she ever experienced. She couldn't hold herself any longer and collapsed off his shoulders. With one last flick of his tongue him and the other gentleman turned and exited the room, once again leaving Alexis there tied up.

About two minutes later she once again heard the door open and the sound of what now appeared to be three people walking in the room. She was unhooked from the chain that had her upright and carried over to a bed. She then felt someone unstrap her feet from the restraints and before she had a chance to think grab her hips and slam his hard dick inside her wet pussy…

To Be Continued